ROOKIE

Lindi Tardif

WHAT THE CRITICS ARE SAYING

"This book was a familiar read as I felt the main character's struggle with imposter syndrome. It definitely took me on an emotional journey as she worked against the powers that be in an industry that has been shown to be not so kind to women."

–Kenyeda Adams, Black Girl Gamers Community Manager

"Rookie is deserving of Rookie of the year. An accurate and poignant tale about reaffirming your self-worth and finding your voice in a sea of treachery. Mixed in with some malicious compliance here and there, Rookie depicts an accurate depiction of the gaming industry from the inside out. Tardif delivers the uncomfortable truth and gives perspective and nuance to the aftermath of a historical cultural shift."

−Monet Turner, an avid Black Gamer

"Rookie is an absorbing, suspenseful, and enriching story that reveals the stakes and faces (albeit fictional) behind so many headlines and statistics that people may know but not feel the relevance of. It's a story of visibility of employees and transparency of corporations – emphatically suggesting both be seen for who they really are. It's a compelling story of justice and courage, and most of all, a story that moves the reader to empathize, think, and question. An enjoyable and important read." #humanityoverprofit

−Natasha Mathews, Policy Consultant

For Amelia, Naledi, and Abraham.

Rookie

Table of Contents

Chapter One

Changing your zip code doesn't make you visible to the world, said the quiet voice in her head.

Jane Jackson crossed the street with an unconscious caution in her walk, with a reserve that had always been a weight on her shoulders from as far back as she could remember.

The brown sign of the Mercer Island Country Club loomed a few feet away from her.

Her current zip code: 98040.

She trudged towards the landmark sign, effectively drawing closer to the MICC's parking lot with its splattering of assorted automobiles—the black, shiny Dodge van that had to have arrived with a load of swimming or tennis lessons children; the white Land Rover with the American flag trailing on its antenna, a relic from the fourth of July celebrations of the previous weekend, and an indication of a millennial owner; and, of course, always a Tesla, BMW, or Porsche, maybe two, spotless, shiny, brand-spanking new-looking, in luxurious display across the MICC lot.

Changing your zip code doesn't make you visible to the world.

Why wouldn't this thought get out of her head?

Her house keys chinked as she walked, stored neatly in the thin-strapped, Gucci key wallet slung across her shoulder. Five minutes away from her current coordinates, the white, older house on SE 71st street beckoned like a haven away from the musings of her mind: A $2,500 per month deal with two bedrooms, two bathrooms, and a roommate, it was the best she could do on a new student graduate budget. At $1,250 a month for rent, a prime spot like the southeast end of greater Seattle's Mercer Island was the dream of many a struggling artist of the Pacific Northwest.

Her gray T-shirt bore the bold letters "Harvard," spelled in maroon text. Her matching gray tights were a relic from her swim-team practice uniform from college. Her tennis shoes were well worn, but she had never complained about a good pair of *Nikes* ever expiring from its usefulness due to age.

The MICC's front entrance loomed before her as she drew nearer, her sneakers hitting the clean pavement with a gait that made her look more confident than she actually felt.

Looks. She was not one to boast about looks. Frankly, she didn't have them to brag about. Her eyes were what an ex had described as "almonds" in color and shape. She was still dissecting what that truly meant. Set in a face outlined like a heart, with cheekbones cut as sharply as razors, she almost made the "girl-next-door" look. Almost, but not quite. Endowed with a complexion that could only be compared to mocha coffee, her impossibly long legs and defined muscle tone had won her a "Ms. Fitness" contest once upon a time in high school.

Obsession about looks be gone. I'm here to swim.

She looked at the MICC building before her as she drew nearer.

All right, Jane Jackson. New member of the Mercer Island Country Club, you. Good move for your gym needs. First official visit to the club pool. You belong here. Just like you belonged at Harvard. Just like you belonged in prep school.

She drew in an appreciative breath. Yes. Yes, she did.

Changing your zip code doesn't make you visible to the world.

This time, she listened to The Voice. Her mind dramatically whirled away to a time and a place that was a different zip code that she had left behind only a few years ago.

****

Fairfield, Baltimore—10 Years Earlier

Fairfield, Baltimore. Median home income: $29,271. Unemployment rate: 9.9 percent. Crime per 100,000 people—11,128.

Jane jumped at the sound of the loud, insistent knock coming from the front door of 3032 Strickland Street, Baltimore, Maryland. With a crinkling sound that she always loved when handling paper, she stashed away the Crime Statistics section of the newspaper she had been reading.

Her current zip code: 21223.

The draft of air moving through the rafters made the house feel cooler and more somber than usual. The north facing windows of the living room threw a dark shadow of the gathering dusk over the tattered brown couch that she had been lying on. The only company around her was the soft whisper of that strong air moving through the house. She leapt up from the couch. She hesitated.

The door shook with that insistent knock again. Twelve years of living in this same house, one would have thought she would be used to door knocks that sounded like an inquiry from armed robbers.

Eleven thousand one hundred twenty-eight crimes per hundred thousand people in the neighborhood would mean that she stood a chance of being a crime statistic at a rate of about eleven out of one hundred on a daily basis.

The wire fencing that surrounded the faded, white four-bedroom house was of a height of the fencing found at a maximum security prison. The 8,276 square-foot lot that surrounded it, overgrown with weeds and nettles, spoke of the homeowner's many hours spent at work or in idle pursuits, with not an extra moment spared to pamper the yard with loving attention.

Another hard knock on the door reverberated through the currents of cool air that circulated the house. "Jane! JJ, are you buried in your books again? I see your bicycle out here, so I know you're in. Come and open the door for your uncle!"

The strong, deep voice of her dad's younger brother ruled out the possibility that she was just about to be fodder for home robbers. It was just Uncle Sylvester at the door.

Maybe she should stop reading the Crime Statistics section of the newspapers. Or maybe, she should stop poring over her favorite Sherlock Holmes murder-adventure novels for a while to relieve her mind from these horrors. She was likely not going to die from a neighborhood crime-related incident tonight, as the newspapers and novels she loved to read so often suggested.

Jane rushed for the front door and threw it open with eagerness. "Hi."

The tall, skinny man with shaggy hair sprinkled with dustings of white looked down his nose at her from his great height. "Your Mom and Dad are still at work?"

Jane nodded. She broke into a smile when she spotted her Aunt Charmaine unbuckling the toddler from the car seat of the 1988 gray Ford Aerostar. At the sight of the cherub-faced two-year-old who was being lugged out of the car, Jane promptly forgot her Uncle Sylvester and flew down the two steps of the front porch to peek over her aunt's shoulder. "Hey, Aunt Charmaine! You brought Maya!"

Aunt Charmaine broke into a smile as she lifted the sleepy-faced toddler into her arms. "I know, dear. She has been with my mom a lot." Aunt Charmaine had that lowered-head posture that Jane had come to recognize was her way of avoiding eye contact. She darted a look in her husband's direction. "Since I'm working so much these days."

"Will you be standing around gossiping or do you want to come in from the cold?"

Uncle Sylvester's exasperated voice, coming from the porch, announced that he was still there. That he was watching the exchange between Jane and her aunt. He had a point. The temperatures had been averaging fifty degrees all the month of November but much colder weather was on its way. It reminded Jane of the depressing fact that she had just discovered a hole in the armpit of her old ski jacket that she wore to school. She knew she would not be getting a new one anytime soon.

Aunt Charmaine was trying to grab a tote bag out of the back of the car while balancing the half-asleep Maya in one arm. The back of the car was overflowing with suitcases, blankets, and even boxes positively smashed in beside Maya's car seat so that she wondered if the toddler had any room for fresh air while the car traveled.

The inside of their car was always like a freak show of junk paper; food crumbs; knickknacks that included grubby dolls; snack wrappers; and boxes filled with one contraption or another, which always represented Uncle Sylvester's latest business schemes. Yet never had Jane seen the back seat *this* stashed. That was strange.

Pushing her musings aside, Jane held out her arms. "Here, let me carry Maya." Aunt Charmaine smiled her relief as she handed the toddler over. Jane lovingly snuggled the dozing two-year-old into her arms. Skipping carefully up the porch steps, she followed Uncle Sylvester into the house, and Aunt Charmaine trailed behind, her head still down, as if watching the ground that she threaded was the most important feat in the world.

"Your dad will be back at seven?" Uncle Sylvester was making his way up the wooden stairs. It was not a strange occurrence. He came over all the time and moved around his older brother's home with ease. Except, he had never come by when Jane's dad or mother were not around. It was like a silent rule that the family had. Jane was not quite sure of the origins of that rule, only that her dad's testy temper would often flare at the mention of his younger brother dropping by when he was not home. Strange indeed.

Jane nodded in response to Uncle Sylvester's question, but when she remembered that his back was turned as he got to the landing at the top of the stairs and turned towards the guest bedroom, she responded vocally instead, "Yes, sir."

What was he *doing*?

He had turned into the bedroom of Jane's older brother, Julius. Julius was away at college at Virginia Tech. Aunt Charmaine was following sheepishly, entering the room behind Uncle Sylvester.

"Ja-a-n!" screamed a toddler's voice in Jane's ear. Jane jumped and chuckled, looking down at the delighted face of the young child she was carrying. Maya was wide-awake. Her bright eyes indicated that she had been up from her semi-sleeping state for at least a minute while Jane was not paying attention.

The waft of baby oil scent in the child's hair gave away her recent bath.

Maya knew her as J-a-a-n. Each sound drawn out. It was good enough for Jane.

"Yes! Yes, Maya! It's your *Jaan-Jaan*! I'm your *Jaan-Jaan*!" She pressed a loud, airy kiss on Maya's chubby cheek, which made the toddler giggle.

Maya gazed at Jane's lips with fascination as she kissed her cheeks with noisy pecks and chortled gibberish at her. Jane turned to her uncle and his wife for a moment to confirm, "Are you spending the night?" Jane could not hide her ever active curiosity anymore. Unanswered questions just were not permitted in her psyche. She always had to know. Pretending not to look at the stuffed tote bag that Aunt Charmaine had placed on Julius's bed, she continued to chortle and make hand signals at the toddler with her free hand.

Aunt Charmaine's voice burst into the silence that followed as if she had been waiting for the question. "We lost our apartment and Syl thinks your dad will let us stay here," she spoke rapidly.

Uncle Sylvester's eyes flashed at her like red hot peppers. "You want to tell my niece all of our deep, dark secrets while you are at it?" He took a step towards his wife, his bigger size making her five-foot-four frame look dwarfish.

Jane knew Uncle Syl and Aunt Charmaine's story well. They had lived together for a year until Aunt Charmaine discovered she was pregnant three years ago. Nine months later, she had Maya. Jane could still not fathom how the pregnancy arrangement had helped them decide that they wanted to get married. Was that the magic formula: shack up and marry; or shack up, get pregnant, then get married?

Jane was twelve years old this year, nine when her uncle and Aunt Charmaine had eventually decided to tie the knot. She did not understand these nuances. All she knew was that Aunt Charmaine had never looked more miserable since that month when they said, "I do." Maybe couples' characters changed once they had walked down the aisle and after they were done pretending to be married, their "test drive" phase having proved not to have been an accurate test after all.

"I'm your niece, Uncle Syl," Jane piped up quickly, her eyes on Aunt Charmaine, afraid for her. "You can tell me anything."

"'You're a child," Uncle Sylvester snapped at her. "You don't need to be told adult things."

"Jane!" a door slammed and a voice bellowed simultaneously downstairs.

Relieved not to have to provide an answer to Uncle Syl's testy voice, Jane spun on her heels and ran down the stairs towards her dad's voice. He had arrived from work earlier than expected today. He usually breezed in with the cooler fall winds of the late evening hours, anytime from 7 p.m. on every evening.

The frown that burrowed down the center of his forehead made Jane aware of what he was about to ask her. He had seen Uncle Sylvester's car outside. Perhaps, he saw the backseat filled with all of Uncle Sylvester's and Aunt Charmaine's belongings, too. She knew she would not have to spell out what she had just heard Aunt Charmaine blurting out.

"Where's that deadbeat?" he bellowed.

Qualification was not required for who he was referring to. Still, Jane debated whether "deadbeat" was a nickname of fondness that her dad called his younger brother. Given that Uncle Sylvester had been to prison twice and already had three children from three different women before he married Aunt Charmaine, with each child not receiving the proper child support entitled to them, she discerned that maybe it was not a term of endearment.

Jane pointed upstairs with her free hand. Her dad moved past her towards the stairs. She did not fail to notice that he pressed a gentle hand on Maya's soft head as if in greeting to the little child before he proceeded to climb up the stairs to deal with his brother.

A volley of raised voices followed. Jane did not dare climb back upstairs to witness the exchange of curse words from her dad and responses intended as guilt trips, fired back by Uncle Sylvester.

"You are not staying in my house!" Joe yelled. "Everyone in the family is tired of your parasitic behind, Syl! You move in and never leave!"

"That's not true, Joe!" Uncle Sylvester shouted back.

"Yeah? Remind me how long you stayed with Gloria and her husband before they had to kick your behind out of their house?"

"Joe, you, of *all* people, should know my situation. You are my big brother, man. I'm in a bit of a bind. You've been there before. You had to live with our oldest brother, Peter, when you and Clara didn't have a place to stay while she was pregnant, remember?"

Jane's ears perked up. All right. She had heard about the story of her mom, Clara, and her dad, Joe, being homeless for a while in the year that Jane had been born. She knew that homelessness was not a new story in the Jackson family. It was probably the reason she was puzzled about her dad's reaction to Uncle Sylvester's staying with them.

She sank down onto the couch where she had gotten up from almost a lifetime ago, placing the silent Maya beside her. The little girl looked up at her expectantly, a small smile on her face, as if she was waiting to be entertained.

The voices continued to bellow upstairs.

Jane kissed Maya's forehead. The little child looked up at her with a toothy grin and held up her pinky finger, then her thumb and her index finger, while the rest of her fingers, her middle and ring fingers pressed down against her palm.

Tears stung Jane's eyes, "I love you, too, Maya." She signaled back to the child.

She turned her face away from the two-year-old so that Maya could not read her lips. "I'm so glad you cannot hear the quarrel going on upstairs with my dad and your parents right now, sweet Maya."

Chapter Two

Present Day—Mercer Island Country Club

You are a frigging Harvard Law graduate, Jane Jackson. Growing up in a little shack in Baltimore does not disqualify you from going into MICC like you own it!

What had made her hesitate to go in at the precise minute that she had only to breeze through the front entrance of the club?

Like the couple that was just walking out the doors, looking like Wimbledon athletes just coming off the tennis court. Well-to-do Wimbledon athletes.

They looked like they belonged here. She with a mane of silky dark hair that flowed in perfect smoothness to her shoulders, arching a couple of inches below her chin in the stylish new long bob that was the rave this summer. Her white, mid-rise skirt, worn over a high-neck Racerback, matching white tank top, and Nikes screamed super model chic. Her male companion followed closely behind her in black tennis shorts and a white Nike polo shirt and black sneakers.

"Why would you want me to say hello to my cousin next time I see her? Do you like her? Is that why she wanted me to say hello to you?"

Jane froze. She took proper stock of the couple walking through the door where she had been standing just at the entrance, her earlier hesitation at entering the club seemingly invisible to the objective eye, but to her it had been there. Her admiration of their trendy style had been a little superficial. She had not seen the miserable look that the guy was sporting as he followed his chic girlfriend out of the club. *What the heck had the lady just said to her guy?*

"Tanya, don't be ridiculous," he gestured with one hand, palm up, as if to describe his helplessness. "I don't like your cousin-slash-best friend. I mean, not the way you think." He stopped with a rush of frustrated breath and seemed to notice that Jane was standing by the door, waiting for them to walk through so that she could slip in. Politely, he stepped aside, allowing her to pass him and enter the building. He did look positively dismal.

Jane smiled her thanks and walked by them, ears perked. She could still hear the girl's speech.

"You can ask her out if you want, you know." The lady called Tanya didn't appear mindful of the reach of her voice or that she sounded like a jealous banshee.

Her boyfriend mumbled something out of Jane's hearing as he hurried after her, seemingly still trying to pacify her. Jane paused in the entrance for a moment, a reflective frown on her brow. She had thought the crazy-jaundiced girlfriend type was *so* college campus.

Leaving Harvard and coming out into the big bad world had made her apprehensive, especially in these past couple of months since her law school graduation. Going back to Baltimore had been the comfortable option. Her parents still lived there and home was, well, safe. She would not have to put in any work to be seen or recognized in anything she did. Her family and community fawned over her well enough for being the first and only one in all the generations of the Jackson family who had ever gone to an Ivy League school.

How did her sighting of the yuppie guy and his girlfriend relate to her musings about being an imposter Mercer Islander who was trying to fit in at the local country club? Maybe it was a reminder that she was not the only one with insecurities. White, yuppie girlfriends in expensive tennis gear and very likely sporting a sizable trust fund had some massive insecurity issues, too.

She was good to go into MICC for her swim now. Jane breezed in, heading towards the swimming pool area.

****

Palms touched the water. Legs straight. Her balance began to give way, as she had intended. She leapt lightly. *Splash!* Her body stretched in the water for three to five seconds before she moved. Arms performing semi-circular movements, her legs achieving frog kicks, she breathed freely. She kept her eyes open.

Well done, Jane Jackson.

It was her perfect "pretend-amateur" dive that demonstrated the prowess of an expert. She could tell.

The kids sitting to the east corner of the swimming pool were staring with awe.

Finish the race.

The Voice suddenly reverberated in her mind. She knew that voice.

Stand tall and stand proud.

His voice in her head again.

She reached the end of the pool and kicked back against the wall with her foot, propelling her body back in a smooth glide in the direction she had just come from, her arms cutting through the water in the semi-circular arcs of the breaststroke.

Be unapologetic.

Declan Anderson's voice was like a recording playing through her mind. A voice from graduation.

A lawyer. An influencer. The man behind the modern-day civil rights movement for Black professionals. The man she had followed in all her days of high school who was the reason behind her decision to go to law school. The man who had been invited to this year's Harvard Law School graduation as the keynote speaker to her graduating class, the Blacks' Commencement at Harvard.

"What an absolute ruckus!" Comments had exploded on social media about this year's graduation ceremony. "Harvard is now allowing a separate graduation ceremony for Black students? Did MLK not fight hard against these acts of segregation?"

"Get your facts straight!" another post had replied to the commentaries that had exploded about this news. "The event was organized by the Black students and not Harvard. It is open to people of any race to attend."

Jane was hardly active on social media. She read; she did not post. She had been amused by the zealous debates about why Harvard should allow such a thing. Secretly, she was glad that it had been permitted.

Declan Anderson was her hero. She had never met him in person until graduation day.

She pushed at the wall of the pool with her foot and arched her arms as she stroked back in the opposite direction. His voice, his message at the ceremony, continued to resound in her mind with each stroke of her arms, with each kick of her feet through the satin smoothness of the water.

He had stood at the podium at the Sanders Theatre, one of the biggest spaces at Harvard, sitting 1,000 people. The graduating class of approximately 1,200 students who would be attending made it an obvious deduction that it would be standing room only.

Jane remembered watching with awe from her perch at her luckily procured seat halfway at the center of the auditorium. She had arrived an hour early to get the spot. The 53-year-old activist had looked out over the gathering with the trademark solemnity in his gaze and a tightness to his lips as he seemed to ponder his every word before he spoke, even when he was delivering prepared speeches.

"Stand tall. And stand proud," he had repeated the words he had said almost twenty seconds earlier, keeping the audience enthralled with his long pause. "Four hundred years ago. Four hundred years ago, you would have lived in an America where you worked on a plantation without pay and taught your children nothing more than how to plant corn or sweep and cook."

Stroke. Stroke. Splash. Jane's body glided backwards as she turned back like an eel towards the opposite direction of the pool.

"Four hundred years ago, you would have to hide behind barns or meet your tutor secretly if, so help you God, you wanted to learn how to read and write." He looked out at the packed auditorium of the sea of Black faces with a splattering of allies of other skin complexions. "Four hundred years ago, you were without a voice."

Splash! Stroke. Glide. She dominated the pool. No one else dared to enter her realm as she expertly sailed like an eagle coasting in the heights of the air.

"Today," said Declan Anderson, his voice rising in a dramatic crescendo, "you are law graduates, not plantation workers. You are learned scholars, not destitute slaves whose best hope of an education is to learn the alphabets. Today, you are one of the strongest voices in America. You are Harvard law graduates. Soon to be armed with the license to change laws and the authority to become officers of the court and demonstrate power in a society that deems us an impotent and invisible minority. Therefore, my fellow graduates, stand tall and stand proud."

Standing ovation.

Water sloshed around Jane. She was back at the MICC. In the pool. Lost in her reverie of graduation day. Ignoring the ogling eyes of the school children sitting across the deck.

Stroke. Glide. Slush!

Dripping. She rose out of the swimming pool, a statuesque, lithe form in a one-piece black swimsuit with the insignia "H" stamped against the left side.

The eyes and mouths of the pack of kids sitting to the east side of the pool area were wide open, gaping at her.

"Is she, like, a Navy seal?" she heard one boy whisper to another.

Jane sauntered out of the swimming area.

Standing tall. Standing proud.

****

"Hello?"

Jane slung her tote bag containing her wet swimsuit over her shoulder as she made her way towards the main exit of MICC.

"Jane Jackson?" It was a vaguely familiar female voice on the other end.

"This is she." Jane walked across the parking lot that was filling up for some evening event that was going to take place at MICC tonight. She had seen the signs that would point the guests in the direction of the appropriate meeting area. Maybe she should consider crashing it. To test out her new awakening of standing tall. Just a random test of audacity.

Nah.

"Jane Jackson, this is Tracey Valentini. You interviewed last week for the level 6 role of HR Generalist with us at Gaming, Inc."

Jane stood stone still in the middle of the parking lot. Her heart slammed against her ribcage. Her palms were suddenly sweaty.

Gaming, Inc.? Gaming, Inc. was calling her back? Gaming Inc., the multinational game developer and distribution, Fortune 500, and S&P 500 member company where anyone who was anyone in Seattle worked or wished to work?

"Jane, I wanted to, first and foremost, thank you for coming in to meet with us. I know it was a gruesome experience." She gave a small chuckle.

Jane tried to relax. Well, she had met Tracey in person. She was *not* that intimidating, but she was only one of a handful of level 7 senior managers in the HR department.

"We would like to offer you the position as HR Generalist, Jane."

Jane blinked, "I'm sorry ..." Why was she apologizing? What the heck was wrong with her? Could she not have started the sentence with something more poised like, "*Yeah, I'm thrilled*"? She said, instead, "You mean, I got the job?"

"Yes, Jane. You got the job."

A silent scream. She lifted her arms above her head and yelped silently to the skies to ensure that the woman on the other end did not hear. It earned her a couple of weird looks from the two women who were just getting out of a car in the parking lot. She did not care. Jane placed the phone back to her ear. She composed herself. Poise, Jane Jackson, poise. "That's amazing. I'm very pleased to hear it. Thank you for giving me the good news."

"Jane, I'm the one who is most pleased." Tracey's voice was relaxed and there seemed to be a smile in her tone. "We are very lucky to have such high talent like yourself in our hiring pool. So that's a yes, as in, you are accepting the offer, Jane?"

Had she not been clear enough? Maybe she had played it too cool in her response. Jane was not so sure if this poise maneuver was effective. Then she added, "Yes!"

"Good," Tracey sounded pleased. "We look forward to getting your signed acceptance. For now, though, this brings to mind a question that reverberated through our interview loop. Jane, you're a Harvard Law graduate. Why do you want to start your career as an HR specialist?"

Jane paused at the corner of the street, not trusting herself to cross at this very moment. She may get run over, considering the state of excitement in her soul. "Tracey, I've known far too many people without jobs and, in instances where they had jobs, without meaningful career direction. I'm talking about folks in my family and community. I know, based on those experiences, how horrible and debilitating to people's psyche that can be. From the moment I became aware of this, I decided that I was going to do something that would impact the trajectory of people's careers and help them to be positioned for success. I chose this career, rather than one in the legal field, because it's what would make me most fulfilled."

A silence followed. Jane almost thought she had lost the call until Tracey's voice spoke over the line again. "That is ... very noble."

Jane was not sure if "noble" was what she would call it. She just wanted to be helpful and effective.

"Thank you."

"I look forward to seeing you on Monday morning at 9 a.m., Jane. Meet me on the same floor where we had the interview, on the sixth. I'll send a note out to security to let them know that you're starting out in HR on Monday, but when you get there check in with them and they'll get you all set up with a security pass and everything. I'll be sending your offer letter by email shortly. I look forward to getting your signed acceptance before start of business on Monday."

Jane hung up after a polite, "Good evening."

She allowed herself to release her voice into the air, this time with a vocal scream of elation.

****

Tracey hung up on the young recruit and sat back in her ergonomic and, of course, economic standard issue office chair with a heavy sigh. A dull throb pulsed just behind her right eye and she absentmindedly massaged her brow as she closed her eyes momentarily to analyze the call she'd just had with Jane Jackson.

"I decided I was going to do something that would impact the trajectory of people's careers and help them be positioned for success. I chose this career, rather than one in the legal field, because it's what would make me most fulfilled," Jane's vibrant voice had delivered her *why* behind her career choice that was bringing her to Gaming. She wanted to feel "most fulfilled."

It was 8:03 p.m. Tracey allowed a soft chuckle to escape her and fill the emptiness of the office that she had occupied for less than four months as senior manager in HR. She was a level 7. A *senior* manager now. The long-coveted promotion had come through after three years of busting her chops on the sixth floor of Gaming, where the drones and underlings of the legal department were housed. Now she was on the eighth. It was just two floors below the CEO himself. She was moving up. Literally.

Fulfilled. The HR generalist job was Jane Jackson's idea of feeling most fulfilled. "What does that mean these days?" Tracey wondered out loud to her empty office. "This buzzword called *fulfillment*?"

She shook her head and sighed. Well, she was just about to become the line manager of some kid who was joining Gaming to get *fulfilled*. Tracey burst out laughing. Lucky her. She now had a private office. She could be as senile as she wanted without an audience. The kid had a lot to learn.

Buzz!

Tracey's phone was vibrating as it literally jiggled on her desk. *Connor*. The name flashed the caller ID on her screen. She sighed inwardly as she picked up the phone. "Connor Valentini, I already told you that you can spend an extra hour at the mall."

"I am not calling about that, Mom. Okay, well, maybe just a little." There was background noise on his end of the line, and Tracey could guess the exact spot where he was situated at the mall with his best friend, Ted: the skating rink. "Mom, I just saw these cool aviator glasses, and all the kids at little league hockey have them. Can I put them on layaway for the next time I come to the mall with you?"

"Connor, I gave you fifty dollars to spend at the mall today! What did you do with it?"

"Well ..." She heard the hesitation in his voice.

"I hope you bought the kneepads that I specifically gave you the money for," she interrupted, feeling the irritation rising within her. Could anyone trust a thirteen-year-old these days with money? Well, of course not. But she knew she would be working late today and would not have the chance to take him to the mall herself. He needed those kneepads for hockey practice tomorrow.

"I got the kneepads, Mom," his voice sounded whiny, "Goodness, stop nagging me already!"

"Connor, watch your tone"

"All I'm asking for is a little money for some aviator glasses. Is that too much to ask?"

"Connor ..."

"You know what, just forget it. I'll ask Uncle Sam."

"Connor!"

The phone went silent.

Tracey sighed and laid her phone back on her desk, tapping her fingers on the flat surface as her irritation mounted while she thought of her younger brother, Sam, otherwise known as "Uncle Sam" to her spoiled rotten kids, who was spoiled rotten, too. Their parents had never spared him anything when they were growing up. Sam wanted it? Sam got it. Now, he treated her kids the same. Her five-year-old, Hanna, had five varieties of Barbie dolls already, all because of Uncle Sam.

Tracey ran her fingers against her temple, as she momentarily forgot the call she had just had with the new recruit, Jane Jackson, and her mind turned inward to her family.

Mom, Dad, you created a monster. Sam spoils my kids, and I don't have a choice but to let him. After all, he is the only real male figure in their lives ever since that no-good, deadbeat jerk, Larry, walked out on us three years ago.

The jerk, otherwise known as her ex-husband, was last sighted by a friend of hers about six months ago at the Pike Marketplace with a new girl on his arm. Tracey could not be sure how her friends seemed to end up always having a Larry sighting around town. It was like her social circle stalked the nitwit or something. Within a month of that sighting, she got a ping from him letting her know that he was leaving the country that day for Japan on a work-related assignment for a year or maybe more. The louse didn't even give his kids a heads up! Tracey still couldn't get over that. And as if that were not enough, since his left, he was only sending child support payments sporadically. He had left the rearing and fending of the two kids and their private school tuition to her, her unmarried younger brother, Sam, and her aging parents. She ought to sue him for making her life worse than it had been when she was with him or, at least, for the support payments he kept missing.

But she never sued for the missed support payments from the selfish lout. Doing so was just going to take too much effort considering how far away he was. She had a job. She worked for Gaming. She made good money. She was on a good track with the company, thanks to the promotion she had received, but she needed to keep moving up.

Tracey tiredly turned back to her computer screen that had gone dormant in the last fifteen minutes of her musings about family woes. She signed back in. Back to work. She had a lot of proving to do to get up to director level. It would be her saving grace with her needy kids who always *wanted* more and her aging parents who always *needed* more.

✳✳✳✳✳✳✳✳✳✳✳✳

"Mom. Did you know that about three billion people play some type of digital game globally and, in the U.S., almost two-thirds of the population plays video games and one-third plays online games?"

Jane almost expected to hear a very elated return, as if her mother had ever cared about the statistics behind gaming players. She almost expected an excited response and didn't know why she felt disappointed she didn't get one.

The other side of the cell phone line remained ominously silent, even though she could hear her mother clunking away in the kitchen on the other end as Mrs. Jackson prepared dinner. Jane decided to keep on talking anyway. No one, not even Mom, was going to dampen her high spirits tonight. "The gaming industry is huge! It brings in more revenue than the film and music industries combined. Gaming, in particular, has a $65 billion market capitalization, hits annual revenues of about $10 billion, and it employs about ten thousand people globally with five thousand of those being based at its headquarters in Seattle." Jane's mouth made a smacking sound as she applied her lips to the straw stuck in the cup of her super-sized Burger King soda.

Sprawled on the couch across the room, Leanne Rawlings rolled her eyes and chuckled and went back to reading the hard cover book propped up in front of her face with the words "Sherlock Holmes" written in bold across the front cover.

On the other end of the cell phone line, there was another momentary silence. Then the dry voice of her mom remarked, "Sweetie, I think you just recited to me the numbers from my last blood pressure reading."

Jane sighed. Her mom had a way of letting Jane know that she needed to speak layman language sometimes. Jane couldn't help it. She had been living and breathing research on every topic imaginable since she was ten years old, including avid research that she often conducted on the crime numbers of her childhood Baltimore neighborhood. She knew data, stats, reports about anything in society that needed her humble, objective analysis, which was typically everything. "Mom, I'm just trying to tell you how massive Gaming, Inc. is." She blew out her breath. "You're not listening! I got a job offer from *Gaming, Inc. The* Gaming company!"

"I heard you," said Mrs. Jackson over Jane's speaker phone.

"We all did," commented Leanne on the couch, face behind her book.

"*Zip* it, Leanne," Jane warned her roommate and went back to her call with her mom. "You don't sound thrilled, Mom."

"Don't be silly, Sweetie. I'm very happy for you. My little girl, the Harvard law graduate, who can get any *lawyer* job that she desires in any city, in any state, in the United States or the world at a *law* firm but she wants to go work as an *HR Generalist* for a technology company—one that makes games! How is that even a thing again?"

Jane slumped in the recliner next to the couch, noting that Leanne was no longer pretending to read her book. "Mom, like I just said, a lot of people are into that these days. People find most of them entertaining and there's also lot of social interaction that happens when people are playing multi-player video games and that can be very rewarding for most people. It's kind of like going to play games at the arcade but better because you have a ton of games to choose from and you're not just limited to playing by yourself or with a few of your friends - you actually get to play against other players. Anyway, I get that it's hard for you to appreciate this since you don't play games, so I won't harp on about it. Ultimately, I know what this is really about: You and Dad are disappointed I didn't go to get the big law firm job that you have always wanted for me."

"Sweetie, you worked so hard at law school. Why are you short selling yourself by not being a *lawyer*?" Her mother practically whined over the line.

"Mom, I know you and Dad have been waiting for bragging rights to tell all your friends and strangers who pass you by on the streets that your daughter is an attorney," Jane sighed. "But, I've got to follow my heart. I feel like HR is my calling. You know what I think about the impact the economy can have on people's careers. You also know how I hated watching one relative or another struggling to pay bills or to put food on the table because they couldn't find work, figure out viable paying careers, or if they had viable careers, couldn't get any traction in their careers." She spoke animatedly, barely breathing as she ran through her words. "If I can't hand jobs out on the streets, I can help people in companies find and succeed in their right career paths, no?"

Her mother was silent on the other end again. "That's the problem with you, Jane," Mrs. Jackson said softly, and one could detect the affection in her voice. "Your heart is probably too big for your own good." She let out a small laugh on the other end of the line. "So you want to be the career Santa Claus? Is that what your role will be at this Gaming place? Handing jobs to people who don't know what to do with their jobs?"

Jane hesitated, "Um, not really, Mom. I'm going to be helping some of the teams with HR issues and processes that support employee recruitment, on-the-job training, career development, health and wellness, and a bunch of other really meaningful stuff." She worked on selling her mother on her chosen career trajectory: "I know there will be a lot to do in those areas."

Her mother sighed, "Well, you are a smart kid, Janey." She called Jane by her pet name, which had been a stable reference in their family since Jane was five years old. "I know you're going to shine with these Gaming people. So, go out there and get 'em!"

"I love you, Mom."

"I love you, too. I'll talk to you tomorrow when you get back from your first big day."

Her first big day at Gaming tomorrow. A thrill ran through Jane. "Talk soon, Mom." She hung up.

Her roommate, Leanne, sighed dramatically, "So, you are really going to do it."

Jane gave her a look, "Yeah?"

"It's just that, well, there was this guy at my school. He was into video games, and he played a lot of Gaming ones. He got …" she stopped, her voice laced with concern, and the words seemed to stop flowing.

Jane gave her an irritated look, "Well? He got what?"

"He got an awesome after-college job and moved away and I don't know how he and his games are doing," Leanne flashed a befitting grin for someone who had just changed her mind about spilling something.

Jane feigned a shriveling glare at her. Leanne called herself the *graduate from the other "H" university*—Howard University. It was one of the first things she had said when Jane met her after responding to her ad for a roommate. They had lived in this two-bedroom, two-bath house together for three months now, and Jane had never felt more adult and good about her choice to move to Seattle. "Well, you bet I am, roomie. Companies like Gaming are the reason why I moved to Seattle after graduation. They are global, focused on technology and gaming, and known for their diversity initiatives and drive to make an impact in this space, which I really appreciate as a gamer because the digital gaming space has become even more noxious since Gamergate."

"Gamer what now?" Leanne asked.

"Gamergate," Jane repeated, sliding into the armchair across from Leanne with a long, put-out sigh, as if she were fed up with the word. "Never heard of it? The war that was started against women who wanted to reform the White-male dominated gaming industry?"

Leanne's mouth dropped open. "I'm afraid you will have to spell it out, Jane. If I'm understanding correctly, you are saying there may have been some opposition at some point to women who wanted to create games just like their male counterparts?"

"Girlfriend, it went deeper than that." Jane sat back in her chair and looked relaxed and ready to launch into a tale of woes. "Once upon a time, a brilliant young lady developed her own game that was different from mainstream games that were mostly focused on violence and skill at the time, and lo and behold, the response to her creativity was an onslaught of name calling, assault threats, and even being ostracized."

Leanne's mouth remained wide open in disbelief.

"Shocking, right? You should have seen the vitriol that was posted by anti-feminist radicals who called the lady's unintended attempt to topple the old world order a 'feminist bully.'"

"Oh dear."

"Oh, that's not all," Jane confirmed, just warming up to the subject. "A feminist journalist that tried to pick up on the story had to run off from her home because of the threats she began to receive as well. Many who supported the non-mainstream 'cultural war,' as it was being called, were beginning to receive threats, so much so that the federal authorities had to become involved."

"Jane, I don't know if I've been living under a rock or what," Leanne looked mortified. "So what was driving this, protest that women should not be gamers?"

"More like a fight over visibility, equity, and inclusion." Jane shook her head, looking disgusted "Gamergate was the backlash caused by women trying to be included in the gaming industry or, at least, being treated with respect within it. I mean, let it be *forbidden* that women should *desire* to create games that represent us well in a male-dominated industry where females are typically depicted as unworthy, subservient characters on many a game console," she said sarcastically. "It is depraved."

"And you're saying there's been no improvement?" Leanne wanted to know.

"Well, as of today, only about 5 percent of games have a female protagonist. In most games, women continue to be hypersexualized, objectified, or treated as needing to be rescued. It's just as bad on the corporate side. Have you seen gaming related stories on that front in recent news? Did you, for instance, see the one about a female company leader that was getting paid less than her male co-leader?" Jane wanted to know. "They were essentially doing the same job, and she was getting paid less."

"Sacrilege," Leanne retorted.

"I tell ya. It was only when she was looking to join another company that she was offered equal pay." Jane shook her head again, "Imagine being a female working in the gaming industry, a space dominated by anti-feminists who would send you death threats if they think you are trying to rock their little boat of game fantasies designed only for the pleasure of men." She looked at Leanne quizzically. "Guess I dare to join such a world by joining Gaming, eh?" And she laughed.

Leanne was silent for a long moment, staring at Jane. Then, she shook her head. "Girl, I don't know how you plan to survive."

"The same way a fish survives in water," Jane waved a hand in the air. "So I may be new to the world of gaming corporations, but I'm no fool, right? I'm sure I can hold my own in that big, bad place where I'll be reporting in approximately twelve hours from now."

"Better you than me, girlfriend," Leanne declared.

"Hey, it's not like this is news to me or to anybody," Jane reasoned. "Most people who are not into it would still know a little bit about the gaming industry: It is male dominated and women only started breaking in after the launch of mobile phones made it more accessible."

"I don't know why they bother," Leanne sounded bored. "If the men-folk want to keep their little Nintendo toys to themselves, let them have it."

"Well, I disagree," Jane said vehemently. "They can have their toys, but they shouldn't be using women *as* the toys, right? You must have seen some of those game ads—female characters are depicted as sex objects. Have you seen the scanty, clingy cloth things they put on those ladies in the games? Like all they are really there to do is show off body parts, and nothing more?"

"I have not played a video game before in my life, but I can imagine that the scantily dressed female characters probably get called the 'B' word and other terms to match real life," Leanne surmised.

Jane was nodding her head. "Speaking of real life, remember the company I talked about earlier?"

"Yeah?"

"It was a gaming company. So, you see, the bias in the games translates to the industry's corporate culture as well. Women are treated as ..." Jane struggled for the right word, "lesser," she concluded.

"All hail gender equality rights," Leanne said drily. "I don't think I have seen its success yet."

"Neither have I," Jane declared. "That is why women gamers called on all industry players - game companies, developers, publishers, studios, and so forth - to speak up against the harassment of women gamers and to review their hiring practices, culture, employee pool, and promotion practices with an eye toward implementing change. But all they got was backlash. You probably would not be able to imagine the number of women that have been harassed, doxed, and threatened with rape and death because they were advocating for equitable treatment and inclusion. So you see, it was the anti-feminist movers that dubbed it hashtag: Gamergate."

"And their justification for starting a social movement against females who only want to play video games or work with them?" Leanne wanted to know.

"The so-called justification was that proponents for female liberties in the gaming industry were unethical."

"Ah, yes. The unethical practices of violating the caveman pea-brained practices of male domination," Leanne agreed. "I think there is a course in college about that, about cavemen with pea brains in the modern world and how male shrinking testosterone causes low male self worth, leading to aggression and movements such as Gamergate."

Jane burst into a fit of laughter. "You're so much fun, Leanne!" she said, tears of mirth rushing to her eyes. "Suffice it to say, there has been *zilch* change for women in the industry despite all this activism. But the good thing is this: The gaming player base has become increasingly more diverse. Women now make up about 46 percent of the gaming community."

"Of the 46 percent of women that make up the gaming community, how many are actual workers?" Leanne asked.

"Sadly, only about 20 percent," Jane confirmed, "And a measly 2 percent of those females are Black."

"And you're just about to join that ostentatious number, come tomorrow morning, Monday," Leanne noted with fake glee.

"I am not so concerned about that, like I said earlier," Jane told her roommate. "I am more bothered by the fact that as a woman, and a Black one at that, I experience harassment just about every time I play a video game, and I know I'm not the only one. I read of a Black gamer who claimed she experienced harassment at least 20 to 50 times a day."

Leanne shook her head, "Unbelievable!"

"Yup, it's horrific. LGBTQ+ folks, players of color, and religious minorities are also generally harassed for their identity."

"How big is that number, do you know, Madam Jane Statistics-Nerd?" asked Leanne, grinning as she sipped at her cup again.

"Goodness. Over 80 percent of gamers are harassed. They are typically between the ages of eighteen and forty-five. And get this, even the younger gamers, those who are aged thirteen to seventeen who play multiplayer games, have experienced harassment while gaming online—a sizable fourteen million."

"Horrible," Leanne shuddered, pushing her cup of iced tea away, as if disgusted.

"Oh, you don't know the half of it, Leanne. What's even more horrifying is that adult gamers and young gamers alike, about 8 to 10 percent of them, get exposed to White supremacist ideology in online games."

"What, are you serious? You would think that there would be some rules around that." Leanne shook her head for the umpteenth time that night. "This is beginning to sound like the pre-Civil war era."

"You're right about rules. Here's one of the main reasons I'm excited about joining Gaming." Jane had a small smile on her face. "From what I've gathered from news reports, Gaming is looking into interventions aimed at disrupting this dynamic. And guess what, it's all a human resource diversity, equity, and inclusion drive."

"Which is exactly where you are going." Leanne smiled, too. "Your career passion and a movement to change the world. You go, girl!"

"Hey, it's definitely my dream!" Jane stated, "Besides, Gaming has been number one on my Employers-to-Work-For list ever since I started making such a list before graduation."

"As long as you are sure. I just ..." Leanne stopped talking and chewed her lips carefully, as if weighing her words.

Jane looked at her friend and roommate comically. "What now? You just what?"

Leanne shook her head quickly, "Nothing," and smiled. "So? Are we going to hit your wardrobe right now or what? What fashion ensemble will you put together for your first day of work tomorrow? Oh wait, I forgot! There's an unwritten jeans and T-shirt requirement in force there. Well, that's too bad for you, Fashionista!"

Chapter Three

Golf, for all intents and purposes, was a social game that required few commitments.

Jeff Erikson stood in the entrance to the office of Gaming's CEO and Executive Chairman's office after the executive assistant, Amy Murphy, sitting by the door, had confidently told him, "Hans is expecting you, Jeff. Go right in." So he did. And there, an indoor golf game was unfolding, a tournament between the CEO and, well, he was playing by himself.

Hans Husselkus stood in the middle of the poshly furnished, one thousand square-foot executive room. He looked pensively at the golf ball by his feet, gauging the distance between the ball waiting by the tip of his loafers and the makeshift hole that stood ten feet away on the floor of his office.

Strategy. It was Hans's favorite word. Everyone knew that. And calculatedness his favorite pastime. No one needed to be told that he possessed it in boatloads. Jeff for a moment allowed himself to be lost in thought as he remembered Hans's last game of golf with him only three weeks earlier at the Aldarra Golf Club in Sammamish where they were both members. Of course, Jeff had lost. Not by design.

Now, he watched as Hans tapped at the golf ball between his feet. It rolled in the precise velocity needed to take it to the hole and spin into it.

"Bravo!" he clapped, still glued to the doorway where he had watched the whole attempt. Hans did not look up as he went to pick up the ball from the makeshift hole in the plush, beige carpet that ran the length of his office. Earth colors were his favorite. It was the reason why the Gaming's logo was a combination of earth greens and browns. It distinguished itself as a technology company that respected humanity's humble beginnings as a base creature whose crude inventions throughout history had probably been the reason for survival through centuries of harsh planetary conditions.

He dropped the ball between his feet again, and poised his club, not breaking gaze with the ball for one second. "Don't just leave my door open, Jeff. The draft will hurt my stroke's accuracy!"

Jeff cleared his throat as he swiftly obeyed, ignoring Amy's perked-up ears and inquisitive eyes in the outer office. He shut the door and clasped his hands in front of him. He waited. All of Hans's VPs knew the drill. No one dared to speak business with him until he was done putting a ball into a hole.

The fluorescent light glowing from the ceiling was identical to the lights found in every other room or common area in the building, so in that regard,

Hans's personal space was identical to everyone else's. There was no denying the fact that many of the executives secretly longed for this tenth-floor office crib with daydreams of occupying it one day. Of course, no one deluded themselves into thinking that such a thing would happen in this lifetime.

Gaming was a product of Hans's personal blood and sweat spewed in the halls of cutthroat business dealings to build the organization from a garage sweatshop where he fiddled with computers and coding to the multibillion-dollar corporation it had become to this day.

Jeff watched the fluorescent glow reflecting on Hans's pate as he scowled with concentration at the golf ball innocently waiting by the tips of his shoes, as if an inordinate amount of effort was needed to calculate how hard to swing his arm so that the ball would roll ten feet away to the hole in the plush carpet.

"No," said Hans, without looking up.

Jeff guiltily stopped staring at his boss's clean head and almost jumped at the one-word interruption to his reverie. "I'm sorry?"

Hans had looked up from his game. There was an amused look in his gray eyes as he straightened from his famous putting position. "I will not be getting a hair transplant."

Jeff cleared his throat. "Hans," he said, his face coloring.

"See that guy in that picture?" Hans turned towards his desk and pointed at the five by six portrait of a man with a thick head of dark hair with a blonde lady on his arm. "That was me when I was young, clueless, and stupid. I think it may have had something to do with the hair. Don't imagine I'm not aware of what you and your cohort think about my new head shave."

The truth was, Jeff and a couple of the VPs had held some asides about the clean-shaven head of their boss that had become a new feature only about two weeks ago, a change from the graying circle of hair that had crowned his head for as many years as most of the executives had worked there. Rumor had it that Hans's choice to go completely bald had something to do with a young addition to his social life.

Hans strolled behind his desk, dropping the golf club behind his chair.

"You wanted to see me, Hans?" Jeff took a step closer to the huge mahogany desk behind which the lithe, tall frame of Hans was now seated.

"Yeah." Hans pulled open the thin notebook on his desk and the computer screen flashed to life. He did not look up as he spoke again. "What is this I hear about Kyle Smith and a venture called Blue Skies Media?"

Jeff felt the heat prick the back of his neck. *Oh boy.* Did he know this day was coming or what?

"We all know Kyle." Jeff did not deign to move from his soldier-like stance in front of Hans's desk, preferring to stand and face the firing squad than sit and get slaughtered. Bullets from Hans's disapproval was better than getting slashed to bits with his silver tongue if Jeff so much as sat down, which would be an indication that he had time to be dissected to bits. Don't ever sit down when you go into Hans's office. Period.

"That was not my question, Jeff." Hans had still not looked up. "Does Kyle not have a business venture called Blue Skies Media that is contracting out entertainers to casinos in Vegas?"

Gulp. Nothing passed Hans's notice, did it? Jeff nodded slightly, "You could say that, HH."

For the first time, HH looked up fully at Jeff's visage. "So," he sat back in his chair and clasped his hands behind his head in a relaxed pose, "you are the VP of legal, Jeff. Advise me. What pot of *caca* is your direct report going to throw at my legal team this time?"

Caca—the Spanish word for poop. Jeff was glad he kept up with foreign language vocabulary ever since he joined Gaming. HH tended to throw out a few. "I had Compliance review any potential conflicts," Jeff assured quickly. "Kyle's latest business venture will not raise any conflict-of-interest issues."

"That isn't the point," HH interrupted tersely. "Jeff, a word to the wise. It is only a matter of time before that *caca* I spoke about explodes in all our faces if we don't *keep* our *responsibilities* on a tight leash. Right?"

Jeff cleared his throat again, "Yeah. I know."

"Insulate."

Jeff stared at his boss, "Excuse me?"

"*Insulate*. Reflect on the word for a bit and decide what you want to do. And when I say *reflect*, I mean that you should conjure up your memory to the time when you, Jack, and Kevin, three of my *top* executives that should *know* better, had three separate but equally explosive *private* business going on with those females in legal, IT, and accounting respectively."

Jeff cleared his throat yet could not speak beyond the cobwebs lodged there. "That was a time when,..." he began sheepishly.

"I did not bring it up to hear you apologize again about sowing oats with that senior legal counsel chick when you knew that your wife has friends in the company who tend to snoop and gossip," Hans interrupted with disgust. "Thank goodness your love interest and the others left the company peacefully even if it was only after paying through our noses, lining NDAs up, and playing an embarrassingly dodgy game of keeping the news out of the Board's ears!"

Jeff shuffled on his feet, "Yeah, Hans."

"Save it. Now, get out of here." He turned back to his notebook with full concentration, Jeff already dismissed.

****

Outlook Email Inbox

From: Tracey Valentini
Sent: July 16, 2018 9:00 AM
To: HR—All, Legal—All
Cc: Jane Jackson, Fiona Banchetti, Joe Olson,
Heather de Santos, Jeff Erikson, Ilana Papadopoulus
Subject: Meet & Greet!

Gamers,

Come by to the HR generalists' common area for a donut, but most especially, come down to meet Jane Jackson, our newest Generalist! Jane will be supporting the legal team. A recent law grad from Harvard, Jane's passion is spreading fulfillment and satisfaction wherever she can! Why did Jane sign up for this gig? She describes her drive to be fueled by the following reasons:

<u>Straight from Jane Jackson's lips</u>

I've known far too many people without jobs, and in instances where they had jobs, without meaningful career direction. I know, from firsthand experience, how horrible and debilitating to people's psyche that can be. From the moment I became aware of this, I decided I was going to do something that would impact the trajectory of people's careers and help them be positioned for success. I'm so thrilled to join Gaming and I look forward to supporting the legal team. When I'm not working, you'll find me swimming, golfing, reading, solving crossword puzzles, or rooting for the Celtics or Bruins.

If you run into Jane around the office, say hi, okay? Don't be *that* guy.

—

Jane nervously chewed on her lip as she reread her manager's email to, wait, everyone on the frigging floor and then some. She could already see necks craning from cubicles around her and curious eyes looking in her direction. Great. Her first thirty minutes in her little cube, and as if the stares of fifty eyes were not enough as Tracey walked her to her desk earlier, now, there was *this* email.

Jane had clicked on the names of the main individuals in the "cc" field of the email to figure out who was who. Their titles and departments popped up next to their names when she hovered her mouse over them.

Jeff Erikson—VP Legal. *Blimey*.

Fiona Banchetti—VP, Recruiting, HR, and DE&I. *Crap*.

Joe Olsen—Director, Recruiting. *Yikes*.

Heather de Santos—Director, Diversity, Equity, and Inclusion. *Cringe*.

Ilana Papadopoulos—Director, Human Resources. *Yelp*.

Jane was afraid to look up more of the names and titles. Tracey was introducing her to all these top shots on her *first* day? What would she reply if any one of these executives decided to shoot her a welcome email?

From: Gary Chow
Sent: July 16, 2018 9:00 AM
To: Tracey Valentini, HR—All, Legal—All

Cc: Jane Jackson, Fiona Banchetti, Joe Olson, Heather de Santos, Jeff Erikson, Ilana Papadopoulus
Subject: RE: Meet & Greet!

Welcome to the Jungle! We've got fun and games ☺ .

—

From: Larry Dawn
Sent: July 16, 2018 9:01 AM
To: Gary Chow, Tracey Valentini, HR—All, Legal—All
Cc: Jane Jackson, Fiona Banchetti, Joe Olson, Heather de Santos, Jeff Erikson, Ilana Papadopoulus
Subject: RE: Meet & Greet!

You can have anything you want but you better not

take it from me.

—

From: Wes Edwards
Sent: July 16, 2018 9:01 AM
To: Larry Dawn; Gary Chow, Tracey Valentini, HR—All, Legal—All
Cc: Jane Jackson, Fiona Banchetti, Joe Olson, Heather de Santos, Jeff Erikson, Ilana Papadopoulus
Subject: RE: Meet & Greet!

In the jungle, welcome to the jungle, watch it bring

you to your sha-n-n-n-n-n-n-n-n-n-n knees, knees.

Mwah, ah, I wanna watch you bleed.

-WE (Mr. Well Endowed to you)

—

From: Angela Drew
Sent: July 16, 2018 9:02 AM
To: Wes Edwards, Larry Dawn; Gary Chow, Tracey Valentini, HR—All, Legal-All
Cc: Jane Jackson, Fiona Banchetti, Joe Olson, Heather de Santos, Jeff Erikson, Ilana Papadopoulus
Subject: RE: Meet & Greet!

Don't believe any of this dystopian stuff, Jane. No one's out to see anyone bleed or on their knees here. Well, maybe Wes. We've tried reforming him, but he's beyond redemption. We're just stuck with him at this point. The rest of us are pretty cool. Welcome!

—

"Ready?"

Jane jumped out of her skin at the sound of Tracey's voice standing beside her cubicle. She managed a shaky smile as she turned around to look at her manager. What in the world had she just read from, er, WE, and why in the world did it look as though no one was particularly shocked by it?

"Ready?" Jane repeated, "Ready for what?"

"We are going to meet some of the folks that may not be able to make their way here."

Jane's eyes bulged.

"We are not shy now, are we?" Tracey's voice teased.

"Shy" was not the professional image she intended to present. Especially not on her first day, "Shy? Who, me? No." Jane shot to her feet, heart thudding against her ribs.

"All righty! Let's go meet the team," and Tracey led the way without waiting to see if Jane followed.

Jane scurried after her as they walked the entire length of the floor until they got to the west side of the building where office suites were arranged along the walls, each suite boasting of a wide glass

door with inner blinds to allow its occupant some
privacy when needed.

****

Ilana Papadopoulus pushed the call button for
the elevator and waited. The marble-floors shone at
her feet, evidence that some janitor had been at it with
a mop this morning, probably as early as 5 a.m.
Janitors worked so hard, yet they were so poor.

She glanced at her Apple Watch Hermès—9:03
a.m. So she got to work about four hours after the
typical janitor started their day. She deserved every
luxury item she owned. She had *worked* for it.

Ilana got on the elevator and pushed the button
for the eighth floor. She glanced in her Louis Vuitton
briefcase to reassure herself she had brought the stack
of files she needed to review on human resource
policies. She knew she could have worked on the
electronic versions, but she was old fashioned. She

loved the feel of pen on paper, highlighter against words, marking all the important points that needed to be focused on in her thought processes.

"Ilana!"

She froze. She had only one foot out of the elevator and someone was calling her name already.

Tracey approached with a Cheshire cat smile on her face. Walking closely behind her was an uncertain looking chocolate-skinned girl with her head slightly downcast, as if she had some uncertainty bug buzzing around her head about her being there.

Ilana could smell the type a mile away.

Rookie.

She plastered a smile to her face as Tracey stopped in front of her. "Hey, Ilana, Jane and I are making the rounds to say hi to everyone." Tracey placed a hand on Jane's shoulder, forcing the younger lady reluctantly to inch forward. "Jane is our new HR

Generalist, Harvard Law, and she will be supporting the legal team."

Harvard. Well. Ilana's face did not hide her fascination. "Well. I'm awed. Jane, I'm sure Tracey has gushed about how happy we are to have you here?"

"Innumerable times," Jane acknowledged, with a sparkling smile.

"Jane, Ilana is our Director of HR," Tracey introduced, "I daresay, you two might work together, as there may, potentially, be some hiring activity in legal soon. Not confirmed but just warning you!" she said cheerily.

"It would be an honor," Ilana smiled at the younger employee. "Welcome aboard, Jane."

Tracey smiled again, "All right! We have more rounds to make. See you around, Ilana."

And she hurried off, Jane following close at her heels.

****

"Hello, Jeff."

Jeff looked up from his computer in the direction of the open door of his office. There stood Tracey and a cute girl with curly shoulder length hair and the skin tone of his first girlfriend in college, Anna. She had been an experiment in self-discovery. He would never forget Anna. He remembered what his fraternity brothers had called them often: He had been Vanilla and Anna had been Chocolate.

"We have a new recruit." Tracey took a step into the office, forcing Jeff out of his one-second musing. She turned to look at the girl with her who had no choice but to step forward with a shy smile, hands clasped in front of her.

"Let me guess," Jeff interrupted what Tracey was about to say. "I'm just about to meet our new recruit from Harvard."

The new recruit gave him a surprised look, "You know of me?"

"I make it my business to know of all our recruits, particularly as you will be interfacing with my team. Let me just say already: We need you!"

The young joiner practically preened and laughed self-consciously.

"Jane, Jeff Erikson is our VP of legal," Tracey introduced.

Jane looked awed, recalling this from the names on the welcome email she had received. "Oh."

"You will be directly supporting some of his team members—the team that supports the business development folks, to be more precise. I would like you to meet a few of those as well. So let's leave Jeff to his law reviews and go meet the others, shall we?"

Jeff waved and Jane waved back as she hurried after Tracey to exit the office.

"See you, Jane," Jeff spoke softly into the empty office.

****

"Heather! Just the person we are looking for!"

Heather de Santos, Director of DE&I, looked up from the coffee maker that was percolating in front of her in the eclectically painted kitchen of the sixth floor. She called it *eclectic* because the west wall was painted red, the east was yellow, the north was blue, and then a wide glass door set in a glass wall graced the south side, as the exit.

It was her fourth cup of coffee this morning and it was barely 9:23 a.m. She knew what her sister, Marina, thought about her coffee-drinking obsession,

"The human body can subsist without the aid of caffeine substances, you know," Marina would tease. "I can't wait for the day when you will detox from all that guzzling."

"It keeps me awake and useful," Heather would usually respond with a cup of Starbucks latte clutched in her hand. "Don't judge me!"

She felt almost guilty holding her giant mug right now, waiting for the coffee in the office kitchen to brew. Her stash of Xanax pills was in her purse under her desk. She intended to have them as an accompaniment with her coffee. Of course, no one needed to know that. Stress hurts. Specifically, when the stress was coming from a particular irrational being that headed the legal department.

"Jeff, we really need to come to terms on my suggestion to finesse Gaming's Online Code of Conduct," she had reiterated at her 9 a.m. meeting with Jeff this morning. "The current code has ... holes, gaping holes that suggest we do not have solid requirements that gamers and sellers, once we onboard those, must adhere to on Gaming's platform."

The recalcitrant look on Jeff's face had told her she was, yet again, talking to a brick wall in a losing game. "By citing 'solid requirements' let me guess what you mean." He sat back in the chair in the Oklahoma Conference Room and flexed his arms over the backs of the chairs beside him. "You want me to redevelop the current code in a way that will, once again, kiss up the heinie of every low ego, self-righteous, self-proclaimed oppressed individual who thinks that all their problems on earth is because the White man did not give them a chance to succeed in the world?"

Heather's heart had literally stopped pumping. It had taken a full thirty seconds for the pain in her chest to subside. Maybe her sister was right. She ought to lay off the caffeine. But Heather's last thoughts were not caffeine related at that particular moment as she struggled to grasp the next thing to say to Jeff's repugnant feedback. "Jeff," she was surprised that she could keep a level voice, but she did, "it is a necessity. The policies must be augmented to provide for protections of gamers based on race, color, sex, gender expression or identity, age, religion, sexual orientation, disability, marital status, and national origin," she rushed on as she saw that Jeff was about to open his mouth again to speak. "Also, we need to broaden those policies to apply to any sellers that would be onboarded on Gaming's platform. If we do a good job of enforcing them, they will help us combat harassment, hate, and, goodness forbid, extremism on our platform.

"We should also put a team together that will engage with organizations that have been established to bring gaming companies together in an effort to determine how we can create more inclusive and welcoming spaces. HH has been leading the gaming community to understand that we're serious about addressing these issues, but we're horrifically behind the curve and it's drawing a lot of fire from the market. Our users are emailing daily and leaving feedback that tells us they're not feeling welcomed on our platform. We don't want gamers boycotting our platform because we're not providing them with the appropriate level of safeguards against harassment and hate, do we? Just think of the reputational implications of that, Jeff!"

He was already shaking his head, "No, Heather. I've seen the feedback you're talking about. It's just from a couple hundred folks. It's barely a drop in the ocean, numbers wise. All this stuff you're proposing is just going to alienate our hard-core base. Don't mess with the goose that lays the golden eggs, Lady DE&I." His tone was, well, a *tone*.

Where was her manager, Fiona, when you needed her?

And so, here she was, her fifth cup of coffee today, the express remedy to beat the stress. Legal induced stress hurts. Xanax helps. To take her mind off it, she smiled at Tracey's approach. "Hi Tracey."

"I would like you to meet someone." Tracey patted the shoulder of the young lady who had followed her into the kitchen. "This is Jane Jackson, Harvard Law, and our new HR Generalist, supporting the legal team. Jane," Tracey turned to the newbie,

"Heather is our Director of Diversity, Equity, and Inclusion."

"My pleasure," Heather held out her hand, and Jane shook it. "Welcome, Jane!"

"Where's your manager?" Tracey directed the question at Heather. Jane watched, fascinated. Such an easy camaraderie between the two women. They had to be good friends. She wondered if she could ever find such friendships at work.

"Fiona?" Heather seemed to think about it, "Last I heard, she got cooped up in a meeting with Joe. *Nevada* Conference Room."

"Ah. Perfect. Maybe we can catch them together so that poor Jane can go rest her feet at her desk. I have been dragging her around all morning." She turned to Jane and explained in orientation-like detail, "Just FYI, the conference rooms in this building are named after the States of our great country."

"Who are Fiona and Joe?" Jane felt the need to prepare herself before she was hit with another introduction to another high-level executive. Truth be told, a thrill was rushing through her. She had never expected this. Who introduced newbies to executives these days? It was not like she was *that* important. Right?

"Joe Olsen is in recruiting," Tracey explained as she walked briskly down the hallway, Jane rushing after her. "He is a level 8 director and the Head of Recruiting" she said. "Fiona Banchetti is the VP of Recruiting, HR, and DE&I and is Joe, Heather, and Ilana's manager, so she is the manager of *my* manager." She smiled.

Jane felt herself gulp nervously.

"Fiona. Joe. Hi!" Tracey waved at the two individuals who had just stepped into the hallway through a door at the other end. "I have introductions to make!"

"Let me guess," Fiona said in a friendly tone, "we are going to meet Jane, in line with your email this morning."

Jane blushed but she knew the rush of blood to her face was not visible. Exactly how she felt. These big names all around her; she was just an *irrelevant* HR Generalist, wasn't she?

"That's right!" Tracey said to Fiona. Joe smiled quietly, observing the newbie with a downcast face. "Fiona, Joe, meet Jane. Our new HR generalist. From Harvard."

Like *Harvard* was her identity. Tracey had said it more times than Jane had been counting. She felt she would scream if she heard the school's name next to her own once more this morning.

"Welcome aboard, Jane," Fiona had that executive-type, reserved smile on her rouge lips, and her blue eyes were hooded and observant, as if she could see all of Jane's inner jitters, and felt gratified by it.

After all, Jane was in the presence of executive royalty.

"Welcome, Jane," Joe spoke for the first time, the smile still on his face. His salt and pepper hair thick and flopping slightly over his forehead. "I trust you are going to have a long worthy career at Gaming."

Weird. *Long* and *worthy*. He sounded so old-fashioned, Jane decided. Like he didn't trust her to fulfill either one.

"Let us know if you need anything, Jane." Fiona's smile was still in place. "That's what we're here for."

Jane preened, "Thank you!"

"Enough of the intros! Jane and I will head back to our desks. Holler if you need anything." Tracey waved at the executives, turned to look at Jane, and began walking down the hall again, Jane rushing after her. Tracey's strides were truly long. Had she been a long-distance sprinter at some point in life?

****

Tracey plonked down behind her desk and drew in a long breath and exhaled. Through the glass wall of her office overlooking the common area beyond, she saw that Jane was back at her desk, and two or three HR Generalists were gathered around her, talking animatedly.

Well, clearly the girl made friends easily.

She glanced at her watch. The round of intros had taken up to thirty minutes. That was more time than Tracey had intended to spend, introducing a newbie around the block. She had service level agreement deadlines to meet and snooty lawyers to satisfy. She sighed as she picked up the phone on her desk and speed-dialed Kyle Smith's number.

The Senior Corporate Counsel picked up the phone at the first ring. "I hope you have good news for me, Trace," was his way of greeting.

"Kyle. Do I ever disappoint? The answer is yes. I got the approval this morning. Fiona cosigned with Jeff. You can bring four new hires on board for the team."

"Ah," Kyle appeared to be relaxing in his big leather chair in his fairly big corporate counsel office. "Trace, you amaze me. Great job."

Tracey let out a silent sigh as pleasure rushed through her. *Hear that? Trace. Great job. It was the sound of her potential being appreciated.*

"I aim not to disappoint," she giggled. "Let me know if you need anything else, Kyle."

"You bet." Kyle hung up the phone and leaned back in his leather chair, hands braced behind his head. He had the final *go*.

It was about time. *Party* time. He needed the extra hands on his team. His *Vegas Fiesta LLC* was suffering, and the new outfit he had started in Mexico was going to need a little more attention than he was giving it.

He was getting more drones to cover his back. HR just made his day. It was exactly what he needed. God bless Tracey.

Chapter Four

"You are glowing."

"Shut up, Leanne. And no, I'm not," Jane told her roommate good naturedly as she fluffed her face with her make-up brush.

"Yes, you are."

"Will you keep your voice down?" Jane whispered fiercely as she stepped out of her room, her roommate following closely behind, "It's not like this is my first date around here."

"It's your first date with LTRconnect," Leanne wriggled her eyebrows suggestively.

LTRconnect was her dating lifesaver. But she was not going to admit that to Leanne, of course.

"You say it like the app is an exclamation point. So, what if it is?" Jane hurried her steps down the hallway to the front door, mentally checking that she had everything she needed for the night in her purse. Credit and debit card. *Check.*

She racked her brain. What had she forgotten? She needed to be Girl-Scout ready. Her mom had taught her that rule for going on dates. So a well-charged phone in case she needed to bail? One never knew with guys you meet on apps—*Check.*

"I have heard some majestic love stories about LTRconnect," Leanne was gushing behind her.

Ugh. Leanne was interrupting her train of thought.

"Hush!" she told her roommate again.

"So you never really told me how your first day at Gaming went." Leanne was a master at switching topics with dizzying inconvenience.

"Leanne! Really! Like, right when I'm sweating with stress about my date night?"

"Talking about work should get your mind off your hot date," Leanne suggested reasonably.

Jane sighed. Sometimes, her roommate could be annoyingly accurate. "My manager introduced me to every person with a VP and Director title. I felt like a floating start. There. You happy?"

"Aww, sis. Mingling with all the Gaming highflyers. I'm so proud."

Jane turned her back on Leanne, pretending to be irritated, but inwardly, she preened.

It was exactly right. She had been mingling with the big wigs back at Gaming. Maybe her next stop would be Employee of the Month if employees actually vied for that and if she could manage to impress the big wigs.

"Okay, gotta go!" Jane's heels were click-clacking down the house's hallway.

"Don't miss your curfew!" Leanne teased, as she made herself scarce, disappearing into the living room.

Jane rolled her eyes and took a deep breath. Here goes. She was stepping into a dating night. She opened the front door and hurried to her car parked on the curb.

****

There was a quiet, regal air to the tall Asian guy who stood up as soon as the maître d' brought Jane to the table with an incredibly expansive view of Elliot Bay Marina at Palisade in Magnolia. How tall was this dude, like six-three? He made her feel a tad short at her own five-eleven height.

Jane's step faltered about ten meters from the table where he stood, waiting. The crew cut he sported made him look almost militaristic. His eyes were unnervingly watchful of her every step. The ring with the sapphire stone on his right hand was supposed to be a testament to the Ivy League college he had attended and graduated from. His custom-tailored dark blazer wafted with a scent of newness that hinted it was recently purchased. The table in front of him had the customary bread rolls that the restaurant usually laid out before meals were ordered. She saw that he had not touched them. Probably an indication of a guy who did not go for the cheap offerings on a restaurant menu.

Gauge, gauge, gauge. Thirty seconds of seeing him standing there and she was gauging, gauging, and gauging.

Way to go, LTRc, she mentally whooped. His online pictures had done him no justice. Was he really this tall in person?

"Jane," he said.

Was it her imagination? Did he have a slight British accent? Jane was sure she would swoon on the spot.

She did not trust herself to speak. So, she *ah-hemed.*

He smiled, revealing the dimple in his cheek. "I'm Duke," he held out a hand.

Jane took the proffered hand, feeling her palm go clammy. *Oh dear, oh dear, oh dear.* He must know that she had broken out in a nervous sweat.

He was smiling as he waited for her to sit. He sat across the table. She gave him a quizzical look, noting that he had not stopped smiling or staring. Not in a bug-eyed, unblinking way. More like a slow appraisal of her, "What?" she could hardly get the word out.

"You're beautiful."

She flushed. Heart somersault. Keep the focus, girlfriend, she told herself. Keep the focus. "I bet you say that to all the Black girls."

The flash of a grin appeared with that drop-dead gorgeous dimple on his face again. "Ah. You get right to the point. I thought we already resolved questions about interracial dating in our conversations on LTRc?"

She leaned on her palm to give him a full look. "You mean, why is an Asian guy dating a Black girl? That question?"

"Which you asked only about seventeen times on multiple texts before we met in the flesh today," he reminded.

"You exaggerate. I asked it only sixteen times."

"We haven't even ordered hors d'oeuvres, yet we're getting into the heavy stuff already," though he didn't sound like he minded.

"Hey. I'm that kind of girl. I like to know that I'm sowing my wild oats with the right guy."

He fell silent as the waiter came to their table and took their appetizer orders. As the waiter hurried away, he looked at her again. "Wild oats," he said carefully. "Boy, we are really talking deep within the first five minutes."

"If this conversation between you and me were written in a book, the reader would appreciate our getting to the point," she said reasonably, "Scared of the chitchat?"

"I do enjoy a challenge."

Jane felt a thrill rush through her. She leaned with her elbow on the table. "I'll come clean. I'm not the wild-oats-sowing kind of girl."

That made him grab his water glass and take a big gulp. Then he put his glass down and sighed, "I didn't believe for a minute that you were. I think I got that from our conversation on *LTRc*."

Jane shrugged, "I love that app. You don't have to guess the one you're meeting with. You know who's looking for a one-nighter and you know who's willing to wait till things get serious."

He looked at her. "I will leave that question till after dessert."

"Speak now or forever hold your peace," Jane teased, feeling the light mood in the air, even though she knew the conversation was not light. How was this possible? She had barely met the guy in person for five minutes and they were already talking, *ah-hem*, wild oats?

"So getting to know your date is more important to you than intimacy." He gave audience to the subject about his dating motives since she had urged it.

She shrugged, "Don't you agree? Develop a real connection with your date first, rather than get distracted by lust?"

She smiled. He smiled back. Jane sighed, feeling more refreshed than she had all day. She said with a quizzical note, "I can't wait to hear what we will be discussing by the time we get to the main meal."

****

It turned out they were barely discussing and were, instead, laughing by the time the main meal came around.

"You should have seen me when my manager was introducing me to all the big wigs around the office." Jane shook her head, reminiscing about the day she had at Gaming earlier that morning, "I was like a schoolgirl confronting multiple principals. It was extremely excruciating!"

"So you met all the VPs and Heads of this and that? I should remember that. I should remember that you know a lot of people in high places." He nibbled on his barbeque chicken.

Jane glanced at him and was not sure if that was a sense of warmth she felt. She had not expected she would be sharing her day at work with her date tonight, yet it had felt so natural. After all, they had started the conversation this evening with some pretty intense stuff.

****

Duke Liang watched his date laugh as he snitched the last roll of bread from the center plate. *So.* He did have an appreciation for the free restaurant rolls after all. "I figured you'd want me to spare you the extra carbs, since I will be eating this all by myself," he told her.

"What are you trying to say? That I'm a carb-watching, diet-freak kind of girl? Do I look like I'm on a diet?" she wanted to know. But there was a smile on her face.

"No. You look perfect."

Jane felt the heat rush to her face, "Okay, careful now. Would you say that 'perfect' is a feature that you expect for everything in your life?"

He was silent for a moment, as if thinking, "I would say it is what my parents expect of me."

She looked up sharply, "What does that mean?"

But he was not looking at her. He stared at some point beyond her shoulder.

"Duke?"

"Excuse me," he said it so urgently, that she was taken aback as he scooted off his chair and took off across the floor of the restaurant.

Surprised, Jane turned her head to see what was going on.

Duke had rushed up to a smartly dressed Asian couple who had just been ushered to their table by the maître d'. Around Duke's age, in their thirty-somethings, with what could only be described as designer labels draped all over their persons from the lady's shimmering wrap and black dress and pumps to her companion's dark suit that was obviously custom made.

She could hear Duke's voice carry. "I didn't know you would be picking this joint for your anniversary. What a coincidence!" he was saying. His back was turned to Jane and their table.

In fact, he did not look back at her at all.

He talked. And talked. And continued to talk to the couple.

Jane felt heat prickling up her neck. Was he ever going to come back to their table? Was he even going to introduce her?

No. He is not, a small voice said in her head.

He is self-conscious about you, Jane. You. His Black *date. You think he is going to bring you around his community?*

She beckoned to the waiter. He hurried over, balancing a tray, "You got the check?"

"Yes, ma'am." he handed her the bill he had been carrying about, ready to deliver to their table.

"I'll pay for my meal. He can handle his," she said with disgust. She did not look in *his* direction. She glanced at the bill, and took a wad of cash from her purse, putting it on the waiter's tray.

She got up, just as she noted that Duke was hurrying back to the table.

"Jane?"

She did not respond. She walked briskly toward the restaurant's exit, not looking at him.

Outside in the parking lot, she heard his voice again, "Jane! Come on! Where...?"

She turned around to throw the words back at him as he stood nearly twenty feet away. "Who leaves their date alone for so long, Mr. 'I do enjoy a challenge'? I suppose I'm not 'good' enough to be introduced to your friends, right?"

He looked both ashamed and remorseful, "Jane."

The look on his face was all she needed to know. She had been right.

"Buzz off, Duke," and she walked on as fast as she could, finding her car, jumping in, and hitting the gas as soon as she had it started, driving quickly out of the restaurant's lot.

In her rear-view mirror, she saw him still standing in the parking lot, a lone forgotten figure behind her.

Chapter Five

"I thought this was a *Sign-On* orientation? Why are there so many people?"

Jane's question hung in the air as Sarah Sanders took a full minute to look at Jane and grin at her with the air of empathy that said, "Oh, you poor and clueless newbie."

Jane waited for it. *Here comes another lecture.* Sarah, a big-blue-eyed, Brooklyn transplant in Seattle, and also Jane's knowledgeable Gaming buddy, was going to lay on some noob-wisdom again.

They were seated right-center in the five-hundred people capacity auditorium located on the third floor of Venus, Gaming's main glass tower building. Across this particular main Gaming campus, there was another building called Pluto. Jane had not been in that one. It was on her to-do list to explore this week. Besides these, there were five other Gaming buildings within a five-mile radius of Venus and Pluto.

The Venus auditorium was full. Standing room only. Jane could not understand this. If this meeting was an orientation for new employees that had just been onboarded at Gaming, how was it possible that five hundred plus people were here? Had Gaming onboarded *five hundred people* since its last orientation, which, when Jane looked at the HR schedule she had access to in her department, took place only two months ago!

"My dear Jane," Sarah sighed, and patted her companionably on the back. This was Jane's second week at Gaming. Sarah was not just her noob-buddy; she was her "cubbie" buddy, meaning she sat at the desk, made out of a door, right across from Jane. It was no surprise that they were now having lunch together practically every day. Sarah was cute.

Literally. At five feet three, she had chestnut hair and freckles that made her the quintessential Judy Garland of the Dorothy, *Wizard of Oz* fame, since she loved to wear *all things blue* so often. Today, her sky-blue blazer over jeans made her flaming red hair stand out even more against the brightness of her clothing, "Here goes another crash course in Gaming 101." Sarah took a deep breath as if bracing herself to deliver a nugget of ancient wisdom. Then she looked at Jane again. "Anytime an orientation is chaired by HH, *everybody* turns up. There are many butt kissers who have been dying to corner HH in the same room, and this is the perfect pond for all to capture the frog, princess," Jessica announced.

Jane gave her a quizzical, very familiar, confused look, something she had been doing often for the past two weeks. "Who is HH?"

Sarah shook her head, "*Oy vey*! My job as your buddy is a very exacting one, kiddo," then she announced, "HH, my dear, is Hans Husselkus. Please tell me you know who that is."

Jane's eyes widened, "Oh, of course. Our CEO. I suppose he doesn't mind being called HH. How did I not know that he was going to be chairing today's orientation? We organize these events, as HR, so I should have heard. Shouldn't there have been a memo?"

"Ah yes, *that*. It dropped through the grapevine about twenty minutes ago that instead of Fiona, Hans will be leading the noob orientation today. I'm sure someone sent an HH-is-leading-the-orientation email that we would have seen if we'd checked our phones. It happens sometimes. HH shows up suddenly for talks, and everyone rearranges their schedules to make sure they're here."

Jane settled in her seat, feeling an uncanny excitement weaving through her belly. She was going to hear the CEO speak in person? She had not expected it. This was more "in" than she could ever have hoped for in just two weeks of joining a global gaming technology company. An in-person conference with the CEO leading? Gaming must have some making-people-feel-relevant policy somewhere. She felt warm on the inside.

There he was.

All eyes had turned to the front of the auditorium as people started flying to any unoccupied looking seats, and the mumble of voices began to die down as lights dimmed. The lone man that strode across the large stage in front of the auditorium had to be only one inch short of six feet with the glow of the diming fluorescent lights reflecting on his clean-shaven pate. The light brown tweed jacket over dark khakis that he wore gave him the look of classic tailoring, a man who was not trying too hard to look fashionably put together, and yet, succeeding in achieving it very well.

The microphone squealed in a low protest as he adjusted it on his lapel, someone in I.T. apparently working on the volume levels.

"Uh-oh. Someone's getting fired for that," Sarah whispered close to Jane's side. "HH likes his microphones impeccably ready. If no one's fired, someone's definitely getting an earful from the IT Director, Jack, who is such a butt kisser around the big boss."

Jane gave Sarah's white lanyard and badge a look. "How long have you been working here again? Sarah sighed, holding her badge up in the air. "Just under four illuminating years. Now, hush, the big boss speaks."

"I'm always amazed," the auditorium had quieted down immediately at the sound of the gravelly calm voice that reverberated through the well-amplified sound system, "at the turn out we get during our Sign-On sessions. While it's intended for our newest colleagues, our noobs, it's gratifying to see our seasoned members of Gaming joining in to plug into the newest and latest news that makes our organization so great. Can I ask my team to join me up here?" Then he sighed dramatically. "Is it me, or has someone turned the air up too high or ... is it the buildup of excitement because you guys just love your work and these sessions so much?" Chuckles reverberated through the auditorium. "Well Gamers," he continued, "if you're not hyped up now, you will be by the time we're done!"

There were obliging chuckles as a line of people began to join HH on the stage. A row of elegant black bar stools were arranged just beside the podium, and one by one, they all began to get seated.

Jane could recognize some of them despite her meagre two weeks' tenure at Gaming. Fiona Banchetti, of course, was the VP of Recruiting, HR, and DE&I, the manager of Jane's manager, so to speak. And there was Jeff Erikson, silver haired and slightly built, the VP of Legal, taking a seat beside her. Andrew Smith, VP of Marketing, was a man of towering height and linebacker build, clean-shaven with a warm smile that seemed to neutralize only slightly his imposing physical presence. Jane could not recognize the others who came on the stage, but Sarah obligingly whispered their titles beside her. Of course she named Nigel Crawford, a South African of European descent, and the VP of Software Development; Ken Agrawal, a Brit of Indian descent, and the VP of Innovation Incubation; Michael Keep, the VP of Business Development; and finally Alan Camp, the VP of FLAT, who completed the ensemble.

Jane could not be certain why this particular selection of VPs were keeping HH company on the stage to welcome Gaming's newbies this morning, but she could not help but feel that familiar thrill going down her spine. She was going to hear the CEO speak today. She was really part of Gaming's culture now.

Okay, what was this interrupting noise in her head that Fiona looked like such a lone female up there amidst all those beaming, almost exclusively White, executive men?

"At some point during this morning's fiesta," HH was saying, his choice of words—*fiesta*—to describe that meeting causing a few laughs around the room. "You will be hearing from each member of my V-team that you see hanging around here with me. Why? Because we have some amazing news and strategies to announce. In fact, you are going to understand why we need to grow Gaming from an organization focused solely on developing and distributing our in-house video games and services on game consoles, personal computers, mobile devices, and our very own online platform to something completely new and transformative in our gaming space. Are you ready for this?"

There was a loud chorus of "yes!" among the gathered. Jane's heart raced. What was this? Had she joined Gaming at the cusp of a new revolution? What was this new thing HH was about to announce? She could feel the suspense in the air around her among the people seated all across the auditorium. HH had everyone eating out of his palm. Wow, did he know how to use questions to elicit expectation!

The massive projector on the stage flared to life behind HH and he half turned simultaneously to continue to address the crowd and the graphics that had flown onto the screen, a flowchart that Jane could only stare at and wonder. *Okay, how many new employees are we going to onboard to support this new direction? Always thinking about recruiting and career development for the masses, Jane. Always. Must be my calling.*

"We are opening our global platform to third-party developers who want to distribute their gaming apps to users worldwide. Let's just say we are going to stop hogging our worldwide distribution channel and we're going to allow any other individuals or companies who wish to leverage our infrastructure to do so. After all, we *do not compete with our competitors....*" He stopped and cupped a hand to his ear as if expecting a response from the employees who knew the end of the sentence he was trying to say.

"*We compete with our technology!*" There was an excited response among the seasoned employees.

"You got it! Now, Noobs," he said looking at the crowd, "where are the newbies? Can you stand up? Noobs, in case you didn't already know, here at Gaming we're all about innovating—pushing ourselves to design games and services that blow our customers' minds. That's what drives us. It's what makes us so excited about coming to work every single day. We know that if we stay focused on innovating *the* best game products and services, we will maintain our position in the market. And Noobs, know that innovation isn't something that's just required of our tech guys. At Gaming, we are all innovators! If you're in HR, for example, we expect that you will constantly be thinking about creating better processes, systems, and more to get your work done quicker and more efficiently. Isn't that right, Gamers?" HH spread his hands out towards the audience as if gesturing his approval for their quick response.

"Yes", the crowd yelled.

HH gestured with palms down to indicate that all settle down for his next words. "Noobs, you can sit down now. That's right, Gamers. And that is why we are breaking new ground shortly. Repeat after me: Gaming is VR and AR."

The employees obliged and the room boomed with the chorus, "Gaming is VR and AR!"

"We are going to be developing and retailing virtual reality and augmented reality games. Our platform, one of the world's largest, and our physical stores will be receiving a new, shiny, and sexy look in the coming months as we brand our deliveries with this vertical growth opportunity. You have got to be getting excited by now but I've got more!" Applause resounded around the room and HH seemed to soak it in for a minute before continuing, "Say this one more point with me: Gaming is AI."

"Gaming is AI!" screamed the audience, and people started to jump up from their seats and applaud excitedly.

"Yes!" HH confirmed. "Gamers, business is booming! As of today, almost half of the world's population plays some kind of game. Last year, the gaming market generated over $177 billion, a remarkable 23 percent growth from the year before. In the next five years, it's expected that the global gaming market will cross the $300 billion threshold. If we want to share in that upside growth, we must be more innovative. We must step up our AI game! For us, that means updating our technology in ways that address our biggest challenge of acquiring and retaining users. We have, since we opened our doors, been laser focused on understanding what drives player behavior, and our studies reveal that today's gamers want richer and more immersive gaming experiences and they want to have these experiences across a broad range of mobile and wearable devices. We are going to leverage AI and various visualization techniques to deliver on that. We will be launching AI projects shortly, starting with something we've been working on for a while named Project High. We are also going to invest in AI analytics to get a better sense of player behavior, preferences, and what drives players to come back to a game after taking a break. This will help us gain insight into high performing monetization models and identify further growth opportunities. Finally, we are going to leverage our amazing cloud platform so players can stream high-end games across laptops, tablets, and mobile phones with fast network connectivity and eliminate the need for dedicated gaming consoles or PCs. We are changing the game. Literally. Are you on board, Gamers?" HH bellowed to the crowd. The crowd yelled back and there was a harmonious lifting of hands in the thumbs-up sign.

Jane stared. Okay. Thumbs up must mean assent in Gaming-speak. Normal. That's how normal society behaves. She could relate with this.

"Great!" HH said his voice tinged with a smile. "Our Innovation Incubation and Technical teams have been working with our FLAT teams (that's Finance, Legal, Accounting, and Tax for you, noobs) on these projects and on bringing Project High to market as we speak. Now you know why I've got some of my crew up here with me." He turned around to acknowledge the line of VPs sitting patiently on their bar stool chairs on stage: "Legal; Recruiting, HR, and DE&I; Business Development; Incubation Innovation; Software Development, Marketing; and FLAT. We are going to hear each of their takes on how they've been gearing up for this new and massively transformative direction. I'll stop talking now. Fiona, you want to come up and join me for a split second?"

Fiona, walked up to the podium to stand beside HH, a wide smile on her face. "Yes, we are growing!" she announced, "I'm excited. My directs are geared up for the onslaught of new hires that these new projects will require, and my team is going to be getting sequestered in a flurry of meetings shortly as we prep for this new direction. So, noobs, this is our way of saying: Welcome aboard! You have joined a technology revolution right at its onset! We have a lot of work to do, and I'm extremely excited about how we're going to support our teams to achieve these new initiatives!"

"Way to go, Fiona!" HH declared as Fiona walked back to her seat. "Jeff?" He called up the VP of Legal.

Jane could barely hear the VPs' deliveries from that point. Her mind was reeling with all sorts of potential opportunities as a Gaming employee that would be supporting these initiatives.

Wait, she was mirroring exactly what Fiona was saying—happy to be part of the movement. New movements were good, but when something's new, doesn't it mean new rules are required?

Fiona, Jane whispered, under her breathe, *what about the Gaming community conduct policies? Why aren't you talking about that?*

Jane sighed. Who was she kidding? This was exciting. Someone was surely looking out for augmenting policies. She was not going to let that nitpicky detail spoil this moment. She was going to enjoy being here. Being part of this ... revolution. She could not wait to tell her mom and dad!

The standing ovation officially confirmed her bragging rights. As she zoned in and out, each VP had given a one-minute spiel of their thoughts. Now, HH stood beaming from ear to ear behind the podium and everyone was standing. And clapping.

Jane rose to her feet next to Sarah, a smile on her face, joining the applause.

AI. Virtual Reality. Augmented Reality. Billion-dollar to trillion-dollar market cap. Global domination on the horizon.

The silent voice in her head said, *I've made it.*

****

"Do you have a minute, Jane? Let's chat in my office."

Jane looked up and saw Tracey wave from the doorway of her office. She locked her computer screen and did not miss the grin on Sarah's face, sitting across from her.

"It's the big assignment, noob," Sarah whispered.

Jane walked into Tracey's office and shut the door.

"So," Tracey smiled, looking up at her from behind her desk, "how has your first two weeks been?" She gestured towards the chair across from her.

Jane inhaled and exhaled as she sat down with a smile. "Amazing!" she announced. "Everyone has a moment to drop whatever they're doing to answer my questions, and I have lots of them. And the conference this morning with HH...." She pressed a hand to her mouth and looked slightly horrified, "I mean, Hans."

Tracey burst out laughing. "Jane, relax. Everyone calls him HH, not just his V-team. If you haven't heard it yet, you will soon. And yes, he gave an amazing talk, didn't he? What did you think?"

Jane shook her head in amazement. "Sign me up for the flurry of new hires!"

Tracey laughed again, "You know, that's exactly what I wanted to talk to you about,'" she confirmed. "We're going to be getting some new faces around here, like Fiona said at the Sign-On meeting. And as you may have expected, Recruiting and HR is going to be supporting a lot more managerial requirements. I'm going to need you, Jane, to support the legal team specifically. You will be working with Kyle Smith, Senior Corporate Counsel, who also happens to be the lead for the legal team that supports new business development initiatives."

Jane puckered her brow, thinking fast. "Kyle, I don't think I've had the pleasure of meeting him yet."

"Probably not. He has been in and out of the office for a bit since you joined." She looked away quickly as she said it, and Jane tried not to pucker her brow again. "So, Kyle reports to Jeff Erikson, the VP of Legal. Now Jeff, I think you have met."

"Yes. He made a great presentation today." Jane barely heard half of it, but sure, she knew Jeff.

"Kyle is going to be hiring a few new lawyers over the next few weeks," Tracey announced. "I'm going to need you to support him."

Jane sat very still.

Tracey looked back at her. "Was there something you wanted to ask?"

Jane began to shake her head. Then blurted out quickly, "I'm sorry, I don't understand. I thought I would be supporting employees on the employment life cycle as soon as they get onboarded. Would this mean I'm assigned to support Kyle Smith alone on his life cycle or …?"

Tracey sat back in her chair, her face slightly granite. Jane looked confused.

"I don't know if you had a chance to read the HR handbook I gave you last week," Tracey determined, leaning forward in her chair.

Jane nodded, "I did. Thank you. I recall that it referred to 'supporting management on employment journeys' and so I thought, well, I thought it means the same thing as employment life cycle, does it not?"

Tracey shook her head, "No. We are here primarily to support the company and its management." She gave Jane a candid look. "Take another look at it. That's all for now."

Jane stood up, feeling pins and needles in her feet. She did not realize she had been sitting still for so long. Literally holding her breath and her limbs. She walked uncertainly back to her desk.

"Ready for lunch, Jane?" Sarah wanted to know as she reached for her sweater hanging on the back of her chair.

Jane looked across at her. She took a deep breath and asked, "Would I get a serving of mentorship with the lunch order?"

Sarah gave her one look. "Come on, kiddo." She rose to her feet. "Let's go eat and chat."

****

Jagadish "Jag" Kumar cursed for the umpteenth time as the black Benz pulled sleekly into the spot he had been trying to turn into. Glaring daggers at the yuppie in the navy suit that hopped out and pretended he had not just cut Jag off, Jag slowly began to make a circle around the parking lot outside the glass tower of Gaming, stress sweat already staining the back of his new, pale blue dress shirt and beading his brow. He knew he suffered from excessive perspiration, and this was so not the time for it to kick into gear, just ten minutes before his job interview! Why, oh why, did that bus have to break down in the middle of I-90W so that Jag's carefully planned commute to Gaming, which was originally intended to get him here with thirty minutes to spare before the interview, now had him scrambling to find a freaking parking spot with five minutes to spare before he had to meet with the hiring manager?

He spied a blue Honda pulling out of a spot. Jag hit the gas and went straight for it. He had to get that parking space.

The red Porsche came out of nowhere. It was right in front of him. Its sleek nose began to turn in the direction of the empty spot that just opened up. Jag laid on the car horn and let it loose. The horn blared with such startling loudness that Jag noted, with satisfaction, that the driver behind the Porsche was momentarily shocked into immobility, hitting his breaks.

This was his chance. Jag pulled into the parking spot with a huge sense of accomplishment, turned off the car engine, pulled on his blazer and jumped out of his beat up, white Mazda. He was capable of finding a parking spot five minutes before a bloody interview after all.

With a satisfied smirk, he gave the Porsche driver, who still sat there, engine idling, a slanted, side look as if to say, *You don't mess with my parking skills, buster!*

Mr. Porsche looked like he could use a few lessons on determination. Black hair, crew cut, a rather square jaw, and piercing blue eyes that gave him an almost Pierce Brosnan appeal, he looked too unencumbered with the hustle culture. Probably never had to fight for a parking spot in his life.

Jag did not care for Porsche-boy's parking problems. *He* had an interview to get to. He hurried into the building.

Chapter Six

Everyone loved lunchtime. Jeff hated it. It was the time when he had to play the most avoidance. A time when peers who were after their own advancement would sit you down to lunch and try to finagle ideas out of you so that they could go sell them as their own. It was a time when he had to be pals with board members who came visiting and seemed to think that lunchtime was the most relaxing time to sit and talk to Gaming leadership.

Thank goodness that lunchtime today was none of that. He was making it a most harmless affair. Garrett Wilkes was visiting from across town where he had his own architectural shop set up in the northeast side of Seattle, close to the University Village shopping center.

"You only call me when you need someone to pay for lunch, you old twerp," Garrett complained as he sat down across from Jeff in the Gaming Venus building cafeteria, balancing his tray of rice and curry chicken on the table.

Jeff laughed easily. It felt so good to get a belly laugh after several weeks of feeling such tightness in all his extremities. It had been a tough one. With the announcements that HH had made, which happened at this morning's Sign-On orientation, plus some subordinate *insubordinations*, for lack of a better word, Jeff knew he needed a vacation.

"Hey, you offered," he said good-naturedly to Garett, beginning to dig into his shepherd pie.

"I felt sorry for you, so I thought I would buy you some food," Garrett confessed. "You look awful, my dear friend. How are you holding up?"

Jeff trusted his old high school buddy to be straight with him always, and he knew it. He *did* look awful. He could not forget the dark circles he noted under his eyes when standing in front of the bathroom mirror this morning. Not to mention that he had sprouted a few more grays in his hair within the last three months than the entire previous year.

"If I had to tell you, Garrett," Jeff sighed, "I'd have to shoot you. You know the drill. I can invite you to my good ole workplace cafeteria. But I can't really tell you stuff. Confidentiality and all."

"Oh yeah. We don't want to get you canned now, do we?" Garrett said drily, chewing into a bit of chicken. "So, what *can* we talk about today, Jeff ole boy?"

"A hypothetical question," Jeff said without hesitation.

Garrett hid a smile, "Let's keep it hypothetical."

"I have an insulation problem."

"Keep talking," Garrett encouraged.

"If I don't take care of this insulation situation, a lot of heat is going to come out."

"That would be unfortunate."

"I mean, it's right under me, Garrett."

Garrett took a sip of his Coke, "Same guy?" he asked.

Jeff nodded without a word.

"What's the latest infraction?"

"Three days 'work from home' now instead of one. This has happened three times this month. And I know he isn't working from home. Two new LLCs popped up on the radar, providing entertainment services, one of them in Vegas. The LLCs are using Gaming products for youth entertainment."

Garrett chewed more slowly, "You really got some fire under you."

"Yeah."

"Did you consider what I said the last time about passing him off?"

Jeff sat back in his chair, his shepherd pie half eaten. "He's a good kid, Garrett. I feel like he could be my very own, you know? What would it do to his career if I passed him off?"

"It's no different from insulation, Jeff," Garrett assured him. "You are adding an extra managerial layer to save your own hide; otherwise, goodness knows what could blow up in your face if you are deemed to have direct knowledge of all this stuff. People will be asking if you'd treat some other kid who didn't look, sound, and act the same way as you this way. Do you know what I mean?"

Jeff sniffed, "I get it and have definitely considered it – well before you raised it, in fact, but I just know that he's not going to take it well. I feel for him. You won't believe who has the same views as you though."

"I can't imagine. HH?"

"Yup. He did not fail to mention my past sins with that Senior Legal Counsel."

"Ouch. The blonde chick that was here before Kyle."

"The same one. He thinks Kyle's escapades may shed some unwanted spotlight on legal in general, including that past *snafu* with that gorgeous blonde, Caroline."

Garrett smiled, "I think I know what you mean, but we don't have to mention *his* name. So what will you do? Will you pass off before it's too late?"

Jeff's phone made a loud *ping* on the table in front of him.

He inhaled, "Hold that thought, Garrett."

Gaming Instant Messenger

Justin Filloy (Director, Business Development):

"Hey Jeff, I'm in a bit of a loss. We are getting the groundwork laid out to crystallize the agreements with third-party game developers on Gaming's platform. This is a new project, and I hear your team may be hiring new folks. Who should we go to get the drafts going?"

Jeff Erikson (VP, Legal):

Hey Justin, have you reached out to Kyle and John on my team?

Justin Filloy (Director, Business Development):

My team has been trying to reach Kyle all morning but could not. Maybe you would have better luck. Team reached out to Tiffany Johnson, and she immediately pinged back to say she's available to support should Kyle need her to. She's always so on the ball and such a pleasure to work with! John Putin? Didn't he just join Gaming last week?

Jeff Erikson (VP, Legal):

Kyle currently has John as his go-to guy, so may not be a bad idea to reach out to him, too. Tell you what, let me ping Kyle and have him touch base with you.

Justin Filloy (Director, Business Development):

Much appreciated. Thanks, Jeff and for your speedy review and sign off on Project High. We wouldn't be ready to move into the execution stage in time if you hadn't personally stepped in.

Jeff Erikson (VP, Legal):

You bet!

Jeff put his phone back down on the cafeteria table and mentally shook his head. *Kyle, Kyle, Kyle. How much longer will I have to cover your behind?*

"Veep problems?" Garrett wanted to know.

"If I told you ..."

Garrett rolled his eyes. "Yeah. You would have to shoot me. Seriously, I feel like such a third wheel, coming to lunch with you, paying for parking, going through all those security checks to get in here like I'm some IP pincher, paying for the meal, and all I get is secrecy!"

"Now you sound like a jealous girlfriend."

"Well, excuse me for being the lowly architect who couldn't get a big job at big tech."

"Stop being such a cry baby and eat your lunch, Garrett." He picked up his phone again and speedily typed up an instant message:

Kyle. There is a BD meeting in the Arizona Boardroom at 3 p.m. today. Be sure to attend to help Justin with his questions on third-party developer agreements. I'll send you the invite I just got from him. Btw, he believes Tiffany is very customer focused, so you might want to have her support you on this. Your call on who you want to work with though, as always.

Jeff sighed, "Let's see how Kyle handles this one."

✳✳✳✳✳✳✳✳✳✳✳✳✳

Pass off. Insulate. Kyle. Jane knew she was *not* an eavesdropper. But she was intrigued and could not help listening in on this one.

She was sitting across the table where Jeff Erikson and some unknown individuals were seated, having their lunch. Her table faced theirs directly, but since tables were spaced out at the Gaming cafeteria to allow each group to have some privacy with their conversations, she was not close enough to hear what Jeff and his guest were saying. But she could *see* what they were saying.

Jane chewed on her potatoes slowly, feeling slightly guilty that her lunchtime entertainment was to read the lips of a VP and his lunch guest. But she could not resist. She had played this game of "read their lips" with her little niece Maya ever since Maya had turned seven. They would often go to the mall together, and while sitting at the food court and eating, Jane and Maya would entertain themselves by reading people's lips and narrating what they heard.

It came with the territory of having a young niece who was deaf.

Old habits die hard.

"Did you hear a word of what I just said?" Sarah wanted to know, exasperated.

Jane jumped, coming back mentally to the table where she was seated, her interests in lip reading what was being said at the VP's table abandoned momentarily. "I'm sorry. I totally spaced out. What did you say, Sarah?"

She was going straight to hell. This had to be a gross privacy violation. Jane felt like a louse. Okay, she would not do this again. She would not look over at Jeff's table again. She would not.

"Why did you say that you needed a mentor when we were on our way out to lunch?" Sarah wanted to know as she sipped her coffee.

Jane had almost forgotten she'd said it. "Do you know the scope of our remit as HR Generalists, Jessica? I know I'm only two weeks in and there is a lot for me to learn. But what does it mean to 'support management'?" I thought we were here to support employee lifecycles."

"Ah, yes. You got the old 'support management' introductory lesson, then," Sarah acknowledged, "It is simple, really. We certainly do help out on that front and carry out operational responsibilities such as recruiting, hiring, onboarding, administering employee benefits, training, managing disciplinary issues, offboarding, but we also work to help shield Gaming and its management from various threats. That is the totality of our remit. Pretty straightforward, eh?"

Jane stared at Sarah, "I don't understand. What type of threats would we be protecting them *from*?"

"Jane. There is plenty of opportunity to find out. You'll see." Sarah said cryptically.

Jane looked at her, flabbergasted. "Maybe now is a good time to continue the part of the conversation about my needing a mentor. You are thoroughly confusing me, Sarah dear, though I love you like a sister already!"

"Aww. Would you adopt me then? I'm in need of a place to go eat come Thanksgiving. My parents are traveling in Europe."

"I got your back. So, mentors. I have too many questions, and I know there are some executive-type ones that you and I do not have the pay grade to know. Would you be able to suggest anyone that I could pack around for mentorship?"

"I don't even have to think hard about that one. Ilana Papadopoulous, Director of HR."

Jane blinked, "Ilana. I met her but I don't understand. Is she typically open to that? She's Tracey's manager and a director in our team." The raven haired, tall woman from the elevator on Jane's first day of work. Tracey had introduced them.

"She is like a Mother Bear around here. She took me under her wing when I first came on board, and I think she may be the reason I did not get fired in my first month for failing to show up at a managerial training session because I did not think it matched my job description. Let's just say, I have learned and grown a lot since then. They tell me to jump and I know only to say, 'How high?'" She gave Jane a candid look. "Hey, I'm telling you all this because I know you won't go blabbing to anyone, okay?"

Jane patted her hand across the table, "You know me. I'm too clueless about what to blab about. So, Ilana. Do I just walk into her office and ask, or how does this work?"

"Jane, you can literally walk into Ilana's office and ask. Trust me. She's very, how shall I say, *heimish*. Down to earth and super cool."

"All right, then, I will."

****

So she did. It was 1:14 p.m. on the dot, barely fifteen minutes after the lunch hour. Jane stood in the doorway of Ilana's office and knocked.

The Director of HR looked up from her desk, her spectacles perched on her nose. "Come," she said, even before her head was fully raised, indicating that it was an automatic response. She said it to everyone, without regard for who may come knocking.

Jane walked in with a feeble smile.

Ilana looked at her curiously. "I know you."

"Jane. Jane Jackson. I just joined …"

"Of course, I knew that! Come, come, newcomer!" she waved her hand, gesturing Jane in.

That sounded so welcoming.

"Sit. What did you do?"

Jane sat in the proffered chair across from Ilana and could barely catch her breath at the straightforward question from the director.

"What did I do?" Jane repeated the question, almost feeling guilty.

"There is a reason why a noob would come to my office without a referral from their line manager. And it's usually the 'I need to figure this out' question that gets thrown at me. I'm not complaining. Just letting you know that I *know*," her face was so jovial that Jane could not feel intimidated at all.

"Okay. You're absolutely right, Ilana. Thank you for figuring me out before I had to explain myself!"

Ilana sat back in her chair with a smile. "I know we barely know each other, but I can tell you this. I get the vibe that I'm some sort of godmother around here. Must be my matronly face. Right?"

Jane shook her head quickly, "You don't have a matronly face, Ilana."

"Flattery will get you nowhere. So what's up, Jane Jackson?"

"I'm a little confused about some requirements of my job."

Ilana exhaled. "We don't want that. Confusion about roles could be detrimental to job security."

Jane paused, mid-word. Okay, where did that come from? While it made sense, it was the last thing she expected the director to say. She wasn't sure how to interpret that. "I thought my role entailed helping employees with their career life cycles. I'm not quite sure I understand how we support management initiatives instead. I think it means we police management or support their activities, ensuring that they fall within policies and procedures. Am I missing anything?"

Ilana was quiet for almost a full minute. When she spoke again, her voice had turned serious, no longer the cheery godmother tone she had been using previously. "Did you come across some particular issue to make you ask this, Jane?"

Jane shook her head.

"Well, if there's something you don't quite feel at liberty to share yet, can I offer one outlet where you could air your thoughts freely? Have you heard of the Black Gaming Network?"

Jane shook her head again.

"Take a look at the BGN internal website and think about whether there'd be any benefit to joining them. In the meantime, if you'd like to connect with me, on a once-off basis, to discuss this question or to discuss any others, on a more regular basis, speak to my EA about my schedule. I'd be happy to connect with you on that."

Chapter Seven

Jag Jumar tucked his pale blue dress shirt in his jeans for the umpteenth time. He knew he was really nervous about this interview. Sitting in the reception area of Gaming, watching the bespectacled receptionist like a hawk to see when she would signal that the hiring manager was ready to see him, he felt extremely stressed.

He needed this job. His stint at the District Court had ended last month. He and Deepti, his wife, had just had a baby, and while mother and daughter were fine, Deepti had to stay at the hospital for an extended period. Since Jag was between jobs, that meant mounting medical bills. He could not afford another month without employment.

"Mr. Kumar?"

It was the receptionist's voice.

Jag jumped to his feet.

"Kyle Smith will see you now. Please take the elevator to the sixth floor. He is waiting for you right at the door. Security will accompany you on the way up."

"Thank you."

Jag hurried to the elevator and climbed on board. He got off on the sixth floor, coming face to face with the gentleman who was waiting for him as the doors slid open.

The man's smile froze.

Jag's entire body froze. He was staring at none other than *Mr. Porsche* from the parking garage.

Mr. Porsche looked Jag up and down, "Jag Kumar?"

Jag was certain he would wet his pants. He could not find his voice, "Are you, are you Kyle Smith?"

Kyle's face had converted into a sinister flesh. "When I'm not in the parking garage looking for parking, yes."

Jag stood frozen to the spot. He could tell that there were faces staring curiously at his solid statue look as people walked by.

Okay. What do you do when it turns out the guy who is hiring for your next job is the same one you just cut off from parking in the parking garage?

"I'm sorry," Jag said, miserably.

Then he turned around to head back on the elevator. This job interview was officially over.

"Wait!" Kyle Smith's voice stopped him.

Jag turned around to look at him, with absolute shame.

"Where are you going?"

Jag opened his mouth to say something but wasn't sure what it could be.

"I thought ..." he began, literally stammering.

"That you demonstrated your ability to be persistent in getting what you want when both circumstances and time are against you?" Kyle wanted to know. "I'm intrigued. Why don't we go into a conference room and talk about you, Jagadish?"

****

"I want him," Kyle told Tracey over the phone, an hour later.

Tracey, said, "Uhm. Okay."

"Trace, all I want, when the entire interviewing and debriefing process is over, is for you to give Jag Kumar a call and let him know we are extending him an offer as junior counsel."

Oh brother. Now I have to somehow lean on each of the six interviewers to make an "inclined to hire" decision. How awkward.

Outwardly, Tracey smiled, "Okay, Kyle. I'll be sure to put my powers of persuasion to good use on the interview loop folks. Add that to your Tracey IOU tab!" She seemed to be taking down a note. "Two hires down, two to go for legal," she announced. "Tell me, Kyle, how is the new hire from last week coming along?"

"John Putin. I really like him a lot. He's like the brother I never had. He has a lot to learn, but I'm confident he'll get up to speed fast," Kyle said simply.

Great vote of confidence being bestowed on John considering he's only been here a week, Tracey thought. *I wonder how his team would fare if Kyle placed that much confidence on all his directs,* Tracey mused, thinking of Tiffany Johnson. She didn't dare voice this out loud, of course.

Kyle hung up the phone and sat back in his chair. It was coming together earlier than he had hoped. Once Jag came on board in a week or two, tops, it would free up even more time for Kyle to get his Vegas Fiesta LLC business off the ground. More time when he could put his "working from home" days to better use.

He was not sure where he got the love of hustling from. Was it from his dad? His dad started out as a councilman in their local city council of Boston, Massachusetts. Today, he was the Corporation Counsel for the City of Boston.

It was lonely being an only kid. He had been one all his life, in an upper middle-class family in Wesley. Both of his parents were attorneys and studied at Harvard, where they met.

From private elementary to prep high schools, he was a living testament to the fact that expensive ticket schooling did not guarantee good grades. His performance at school was deplorable and he was not ashamed of it. What could he say? He hated the early school days. Of course, it meant he couldn't get into Harvard, but that was the beauty of adventure. He went to community college and then switched to Boston University for his JD program. He sat for the Massachusetts bar and qualified as an attorney.

Through his dad's connections, he was able to work at one of Boston's premier corporate law firms where he got his feet wet, or cut his teeth, as some would say, as a corporate attorney focused on serving companies in the financial services industry for a few years.

He didn't perform well there, but they couldn't fire him because of his dad, and he knew that and played it well. His dad talked him into moving West and finding a position there. Kyle applied to Gaming and got an offer. He moved to Seattle.

His dad had always been a man who knew how to navigate systems, how to get his way, no matter what. Kyle liked to think that he got that trait from him. After all, he, Kyle, had singlehandedly built up this legal team at Gaming solely focused on supporting the business development team's new initiatives. No thanks to his boss, Jeff. Kyle was the reason they would be adding on four new lawyers to the legal team over the next few weeks. He had created a justification for why legal needed a bigger presence and he had made it happen.

Jeff could not boast of doing that. In fact, maybe Jeff should not be the VP. He was too lenient and he lacked gumption. He did not know how to take and manage risks. Kyle knew he could teach his boss a thing or two.

His phone pinged. He picked it up from the table. It was a calendar reminder. There was going to be a 3 p.m. BD meeting in the Arizona conference room.

He took a deep breath and got up. Duty calls. He might as well go to this one and take John with him. It was about time the Georgetown Law graduate started earning his keep. Definitely not Tiffany. Take Tiffany with him on his meetings? What the hell was Jeff even thinking?

****

Justin Filloy hated being in the same room with Kyle Smith. He despised the fact that Kyle knew almost nothing about the BD space or, seemingly, his own area of expertise, for that matter, and came to every meeting armed with a fly-by-the-seat-of-his-pants approach. Why the hell couldn't Jeff nominate someone else or even Tiffany for this project? She was competent and great to work with. But oh no, Jeff just kept pushing Kyle on his team. He hated that he had only been with Gaming for three years and was already headed towards the C-Suite arena, while women, people of color, and guys like him who graduated from humble community colleges or weren't tall, dark haired, and blue eyed had to bust their chops harder. He made a mental note to share an unsolicited glowing review of Tiffany formally with Kyle and Jeff later that week for whatever that was worth considering Kyle had Jeff wrapped around his finger.

The conference room had all his essential team members: Paul Porter from Tax, Jenny Rogan from Accounting, Jeff Jones from Finance, and, clearly, Kyle from legal had brought a fifth wheel along with him. Wasn't that the new kid on the block who just walked into the conference room with Kyle, the new lawyer recruit called John something or other? What was he doing here?

"All right. We all know our brief. HH announced Gaming's plans to open our e-commerce platform to third-party game developers ahead of review and sign off from your teams. Rather uncharacteristic of him to let the proverbial 'cat out of the bag' before FLAT signs off, but, hey, he's the boss! So the purpose of this meeting is for us to get input on the kind of legal docs we need to line up with these game developers and to find out from the rest of you what you need in order to sign off on this." Justin looked around the table. "Any questions or comments?"

"Yeah, one question," Paul from tax piped up. "Who are we targeting here: local or offshore game developers or both? Also, which marketplaces are we opening up?"

"I heard two queries in there, Paul," Kyle declared, winning himself a smoldering look from Justin.

"I can answer it," Justin interrupted, "The program will be open to all game developers globally and on all of our marketplaces."

"Okay," said Paul, "We'll need to loop our international tax colleagues in on this project. In the meantime, we'll need copies of agreements you're looking to execute with game developers and a BRD so we can weigh in on the tax implications."

Ping! Kyle looked down at his phone.

Gaming Instant Messenger:

John Putin (Legal Counsel):

What is a BRD, Kyle?

Paul's voice droned on. Kyle typed back.

Kyle Smith (Senior Legal Counsel):

Business Requirements Document.

John Putin (Legal Counsel):

Marketplace(s)?

Kyle Smith (Senior Legal Counsel):

Aka, website(s). We have a few.

Justin was saying, in reply to something Paul said, "No, we're looking to legal to help us out on the agreement front."

Kyle put his phone down on the conference table, "So, do you have a BRD on this?"

Someone sighed heavily and said, "No, do we really need to put one together?" Kyle was looking at his phone again, so he did not really note who said that.

Justin looked impatient, "Isn't this fairly straightforward? We want to open the platform up on all our global marketplaces and we just need to know how best to do it. We're relying on you guys to tell us that."

Ping. John looked down at his phone

Kyle Smith (Senior Legal Counsel):

You hear that? It is the sound of BD trying to avoid producing a BRD. You'd think they'd have that bedded down after that rah-rah Sign-On session.

John Putin (Legal Counsel):

Tell me about it! What are these finance guys doing here, anyway? They haven't said a word.

Kyle Smith (Senior Legal Counsel):

They are functionally mute when words are getting thrown around. Give them numbers and this room will be a party.

Paul was speaking again, "Fine, but we're going to, at the very least, need to know what arrangements you're going to execute with these game developers. For instance, will they be agency or reseller arrangements? Also, if you're not going to prepare a BRD, we'll need you to complete a questionnaire of ours."

Justin looked across the table at the legal guys sitting silently, as if they were simply there to be entertained. "Any input, Kyle?"

Kyle blanched. Blinked. Then said boisterously, "Let's take this offline, Justin. We'll get a sense of your 'blue sky' so we can work through how best to support you, taking that and our royalty and other systems' capabilities into account."

Of course, he wants to take this offline, Justin thought, so no one will know how clueless he is.

Ping! Kyle looked down at his phone.

John Putin (Legal Counsel):

Blue sky?

Kyle Smith (Senior Legal Counsel):

Best case use case.

John Putin (Legal Counsel):

Use case?

Kyle Smith (Senior Legal Counsel):

Scenario.

Justin turned to Jenny and Jeff, the two finance and accounting representatives in the room. "Any questions or comments?"

Jeff and Jenny exchanged glances in consultation with each other. Jeff spoke up, "We'll need to see your five-year projections on this."

"On our end, we'll need to see a copy of the TRD before we can weigh in," Jenny declared.

Ping!

John Putin (Legal Counsel):

Is he finance or accounting?

Kyle Smith (Senior Legal Counsel):

Jeff is finance. Jenny is accounting.

John Putin (legal Counsel):

TRD?

Kyle Putin (Senior Legal Counsel):

Tax requirements document.

Justin spoke on, still leading the conversation. "Okay, thanks everyone. Looks like there's an initial dependency on legal and so the next step is for us to sync with Kyle and team. Once we have that and their guidance squared off, we'll share draft agreements with tax, set up sync with tax, and get access to tax's questionnaire. Tax, I'll need to know if there is anyone else apart from international tax that we need to include in that sync. You can let me know after this meeting. Once we've had that sync and tax has produced their TRD, we'll share it with accounting so they can put the ARD together."

Ping!

John Putin (Legal Counsel):

ARD?

Kyle Smith (Senior Legal Counsel):

Accounting requirements document.

Justin continued, "We'll share projections when they are ready, and finance will weigh in with questions or comments then. Did I capture the sequence of next steps well?"

No comment from anyone. Justin determined, "Okay, I'll take silence as consent. Thanks everyone. If there's nothing else, I'll ..."

Jeff, finance guy, butted in: "Well actually, there is. When are you looking to launch?"

Justin announced, "In two months."

Silence. Then came the flood of comments.

"You've got to be kidding!"

"Two months!"

"Come on!"

Justin threw up both hands, "Okay, okay. Yeah, I was just pulling your leg. That's what we'd ideally prefer. We have a mandate to launch in six months. This is a V-team goal after all, folks. If you guys were paying any attention at the Sign-On session, you'd know that! Anyway, thanks for your time, guys."

As the typical end of meeting murmurs arose, the attendees broke up in groups of two or three as they strolled out of the conference room, John stuck to Kyle's side as they headed for the elevator.

Kyle glanced at his direct report as he typed on his phone and walked simultaneously. "Hey John, you'll need to get Tiffany and maybe a second associate to support you on this. I know you're the newest kid on the block and Tiffany and the others have been here longer, but I want you to lead this."

John had a hero worship look in his eyes. "Well, yeah, okay Kyle! But don't I need to give them a good sense of the roadmap first? I don't quite know where to start on this project. Any pointers?"

Kyle had that same blank look on his face that had materialized when Justin had asked him for input about the BRD. No way could it mean that Kyle hadn't known the answer to the question then. Or the answer to the question John was asking now. Right?

Kyle said in sing-song fashion, "John, John. I can't believe I have to spell this out for you. Lean on Tiffany's experience and let her give you all that. Set up a sync with our advisors also so we can get their recommendation on this. The beauty of working here, for us, is that everyone will do the work and we'll take the credit." He winked, "It is the third rule of power."

John blinked, "Oh? What are the first and second rules?"

"Is it me, or do I sense a competitive streak in you, dude? Beat the others kind of streak?"

John looked almost offended. "I'm not competitive, Kyle. I just like to know the rules I should be playing by."

Kyle gave him another look as the elevator arrived and its doors swished open. Before he stepped on board, Kyle spoke again, "Rule number one: Suck up to your boss as much as humanly possible. And rule number two: Never ask him for all his secrets."

"Oh. Sorry, Kyle."

Chapter Eight

Jeff looked up from his phone as he heard the two men walking into Kyle's office where he sat, perched on Kyle's desk.

"Jeff!" Kyle looked surprised to see him, "John and I just ..."

"Took a frisk across the road for a coffee and bagel, maybe a strong drink. Yes. I know," Jeff nodded, nonchalantly, "How have the BD meetings been going gentlemen?"

John looked across at Kyle, as if waiting for permission to speak.

Jeff glanced at the newest addition to the legal team. "John? Comments?"

"Seems like business doesn't like to produce BRDs," said John.

Jeff looked at him again; then laughed. "You picked up that much. You catch on fast, young man."

"I still don't get the full gist of the new strategy, though." John was clearly emboldened by the open atmosphere that the manager of his manager was giving them, "They haven't really talked about it. Only the third-party developer project, which is conceptually pretty straightforward. We need to iron the mechanics out, but at least I get what they are looking to do, in broad terms. What I don't quite follow is the AI-related stuff. Do we have a picture of how this will be coming together?"

"It has been quite a challenge." Jeff looked thoughtful, as if going back in time and memory to a conversation he had in the past. "We created facial recognition and emotion tracking tools that would allow gamers who want to create avatars in their image that reflect their facial movements in real time to do so, but there was a bit of a snag with the facial recognition tool. It couldn't recognize Black and Brown faces, or at least, we kept running into a false match rate issue a lot more with this demographic than others. It's important we get this right because it will allow us, in the future, to develop games that can adjust to the reaction of gamers. So if a gamer, for instance, gets upset and this is reflected on the gamer's face, the level of game difficulty can be adjusted. Imagine how revolutionary that would be? So we just had to crack this puzzle and for months, our tech teams were burning the midnight oil to adapt the facial recognition tool in ways that are effective. Part of the solution was obvious. We needed more datasets, but we were struggling to get folks from this demographic to sign up to our study programs. I'm not surprised that was happening, though, as I believe our guys were only offering Gaming gift cards worth

$50 for participation in a four-hour study program. Who'd sign up for that deal? Thankfully, the guys from Innovation Incubation had an idea: How about we create a game that is attractive to a certain demographic?"

"You mean Black and Brown people?" John said.

Kyle and Jeff looked at him. "That was very deducing of you, John." Jeff's high-handed tone was a reprimand to the junior.

John appeared to swallow hard. "Of course. I just thought I would mention it."

Jeff continued as if no one had interrupted him. "Attracting those types of folks will give Gaming the opportunity to harvest their data while playing the game. It will be a mine of treasured data that can be used to improve our facial recognition tool. Marketing will also be heavily geared toward the folks in that space on online social media platforms, but since it will be executed through online algorithms, it wouldn't be easily detected that we're directing this game more to a particular demographic than others. Genius idea, really."

"This is sounding like a lucrative quest, indeed," Kyle murmured.

"The possibilities are just getting started. Imagine how much third-party businesses or organizations like casinos, for example, would pay for a tool with such facial recognition functionality? It could, for instance, help them detect criminals and prevent them from gaining entry."

"Wow." That seemed to be the only word John could say when he was short of other non-overwhelming words.

"Indeed," Jeff agreed.

"But we're looking at taking it further." Jeff added, "A second part of the strategy is to design and develop game AI agents or non-player characters that mimic human behavior. This is what we've endeavored to do with Project High. I can't delve into details since you two are not disclosed but that's the direction we're heading in"

John glanced at Jeff. "AI agents or non-player characters that mimic human behavior?"

"Yeah, we're designing non-player characters that have the ability to act in creative ways and we're leveraging reinforcement learning to develop AI agents that can collaborate with a player or act as the player's in-game opponent in the same way that a human player would."

John looked awestruck, "Oh, but isn't this already being done with bots? I thought we were doing something innovative, but it seems we're already behind the curve, no?"

"No, like I said, we're talking about taking it a step further, actually," Jeff offered. "We're creating intelligence that isn't programmed to carry out repetitive tasks based on rule-based algorithms. That's what bots do. We're developing agents with simulated intelligence that are capable of making logical decisions and of modifying that logic, based on what happens in the game, as a human being would. The autonomous agents will be able to carry out gameplay by introducing varying levels of difficulty in a game. This will make the game far more engaging for a player. As if that's not enough, the AI agents will also be able to reflect various skin types; mimic facial expressions and show emotions; and engage in conversation through natural language processing techniques. It's a total game changer! The possibilities for other digital products and services are endless and our Innovation Incubation guys are exploring them as we speak." Jeff smiled at his juniors.

"Well, if any angry, Black hood rat non-player character data is needed, tell the tech guys to look no further than our own dear Tiffany here," Kyle offered, sipping from his Starbucks cup.

Jeff glanced at him. Kyle looked back at his boss with a firm jaw as if issuing a subtle challenge.

Was that politically incorrect, boss? His half smiling eyes taunted.

Jeff broke out in a slow smile. "So, you are saying?" He directed the question at Kyle.

His junior did not mince words: "She's Black, female, from the hood, an HBCU graduate, and prone to fly off the handle very easily like most Black females. And have you guys heard her accent? You're lucky you don't have to hear it as much as I have to.

That accent ought to come with some warning sign, guys. Seriously...if the shoe fits ..." he shrugged.

A short silence ensued as they glanced around at each other and burst out laughing.

"That's the operative word, boss." Kyle sipped at his coffee again. "Fit."

Jeff looked down at his phone as if it were a normal occurrence that Kyle would explode about one of his juniors. John looked somewhat shaken. "Um," he seemed to be looking for words, "Thought you'd said she produces good work, but sounds like you don't like her."

"Again, very admirable deductive skills," Jeff noted drily without looking up from his phone.

Kyle lifted his brows as if saying, "So what?" He said aloud, "What is there to like? So yeah, she produces good work and, for some inexplicable reason, the BD guys seem to like her, but she and I, we just do *not* connect. Her communication approach is ..." he paused as if fishing for words.

Jeff supplied, "Direct?"

Kyle looked at his manager. "Yes, we have talked about that," he agreed. "She's too direct. Get this. She approached me the other week about her compensation with a challenge that John is getting paid more, even though she has more experience and despite her educational background being similar to John's." Kyle looked at John with a triumphant look. "Imagine that, Johnny. Somebody doesn't want you to get paid at your current salary. What do you think about that?"

John looked somewhat disagreeable, "Well" he seemed at a loss for words.

Cowardice in speaking up about Blacks? Kyle could not tell but would not put that past young John.

Kyle stabbed the air with his coffee cup, as if his point was made. "Let's just say that that isn't how I would have handled this issue if I were faced with it. Maybe Tiffany would have a lot more going for her if she didn't challenge the *status quo* so much. Seriously, we ought to screen better for cultural fit, guys!"

****

Hood rat. Too direct. Angry. Horrible accent. Not a Gaming culture fit.

Tiffany was horrified. She shuddered at the sheer surrealness of it.

It was after 7 p.m. on Friday evening. The floor had emptied fast and Tiffany was the only one left on the floor as she headed for the elevator. She had to stop as she passed within a few inches of Kyle's office door, cracked slightly open.

The voices were not loud but passing so close by the door on her way to the elevator, it was possible to hear them audibly and to hear laugher from the male voices within the office. Tiffany stopped in her tracks. She glanced at the slightly ajar door, her forehead unconsciously furrowed in a disgusted frown. That was supposed to be *funny*?

****

She got in her modest Honda Civic, shut the door, and sat behind the wheels, unmoving. Her mind felt blank, yet she knew there were many things racing through it. Her manager, his manager, and that new kid, John Putin, really thought she was not qualified to be at Gaming because she was Black, female, from the hood, and she graduated from an HBCU? What did it take to succeed in this environment? Be anything but Black and female?

It was like saying the fairy tale princess, Beauty, was cast during her high school play as a White girl because, well, to be a successful show, the actor had to be white. Right? It was the reason she had been passed over for that role in the production of it during her high school days of playing theater. The drama class teacher had told her. To her face.

"Tiffany, dear. Let's be realistic," said Mrs. Jenkins. "We need a girl that fits the role. Beauty has to be like a Barbie doll, delicate and waif like. It's what makes her story with the big bad beast so adorable, don't you think? You have handsome features. Too thick for such a role, sweetie. I'm really sorry. We just need to be realistic."

It was back in the day when students respected their teachers and abstained from suing for racial discrimination. "The good old days."

If Beauty could only be beautiful because she was White, Black professionals could only be fitting into corporate culture if they were made more willing to leave their full range of emotions at home, less assertive of their rights and humanity, less outspoken about disparate treatment, more grateful for whatever morsel corporate America threw in their direction. Right? The Gaming Logic?

High school had been left behind, many years ago. She had bust her behind, trying to put it, well, behind her. Then it reared its head again at her last job. Five years in a role. Waiting to be promoted. Some starry eyed and bushy tailed youngster from Yale joined the company and was promoted within nine months into the role that Tiffany had her sights on. She quit and came to Gaming.

And yet, the albatross was here, too. *A girl just can't get any admiration for being who she is in this world, can she?*

✱✱✱✱✱✱✱✱✱✱✱

"It's about quitting time. John, why don't you head on out and we will see you in the morning?" Jeff remained, leaning against Kyle's desk throughout the conversation they had held about the latest phase of facial recognition technology. "Kyle, got a moment?" He turned simultaneously to his immediate direct report. John began to head towards the office door. "See you tomorrow." He took his exit.

"He's a smart kid," Kyle murmured. "Learning fast."

"Uh-huh," Jeff said non-commitally. "I leave it all up to you on decisions with the crew, Kyle. And we are going to need to rally them as Project High goes into deployment. I signed off on it but I have been getting a lot of pings from different teams about their own versions of what they think should be included in our contracts with third-party online game distribution platform providers and game studios and what not. I need you and the team to pull this final piece together."

"You can always count on us, Jeff." Kyle's smile was wide. "I know you have attended a few of those talks about the new game. How were they? The Project High conversations?"

"Intriguing," Jeff admitted. "There have been several focus group sessions held to develop this masterpiece. You know the gist of the game, right?"

Kyle shook his head and crossed his arms, looking very interested. "I only just signed the nondisclosure agreement sent by the team managing this today. I'm afraid pay grades like mine have not gotten the full benefit of the genius storyboard yet," he joked.

Jeff ignored the lead into salary talks and instead elaborated on Project High's game story: "It's a virtual reality game set in an inner city and involves the selling of menthol cigarettes by players to in-game kid characters in the community. One of the thrills of the game is that the player doesn't know which kid will actually buy, so they have to get to as many kids in the game as possible and make their sales pitch. Every time a successful sale is made, the player will score points. A player can also score points by recruiting other human players to join the initial player's team in the game. This increases the number of sellers and chances of making sales. When those players make sales, the recruiting player gets a portion of their points. The recruiter is also awarded points for each player recruited. The third way the players can score points would probably offend a sensitive individual, since a few folks were said to have quietly voiced their protests while HH was not in the room."

Kyle perked up. "Yeah? What is this third way to score points? Let me guess, someone thinks it's discriminatory."

Jeff smiled, "You could say that. There are scantily clad women who show up randomly in the game. When they appear, the game flashes a message to the player, reading, 'Tap those bitches.' The player does that by stopping whatever he is doing when the message pops up and moving in the direction of the women while they are running. When the player successfully gets to one, a congrats sign comes up and the player will be awarded points. The women don't have any active roles in the game. They are purely there for the player's entertainment purposes."

"So depraved. I like it," Kyle stated.

"Hmm. I thought you might," Jeff said. "Mind you, if the player is caught by the police and serves time in jail for selling menthol products, the player gets a lot of points for this. So, jail time is good!"

"Sounds right up the alley of some cultures in our great America."

Jeff shrugged. "Someone has to go to jail. When a player reaches a certain number of points, they are awarded a digital gift card by Gaming that can be redeemed for other digital items that Gaming sells, so this drives even more engagement and recruitment of customers to become players."

"Keeping users on the platform. Genius."

"There's more," Jeff continued. "To increase engagement, Gaming will also allow players to play against each other in a virtual league. A leader board will be created that can be seen by all the players. The competition can be for a 30-minute session, for one day, or for one week. If the players choose to play in a league, Gaming will unlock a part of the game that allows them to kill each other in the game. Players can gang up with each other to attack and kill a certain player. Higher points are awarded to players who single-handedly take a player out. If a player is taken out by the gang, points are split among all the remaining players. If a player is caught by the police and serves time in jail for killing another player, the player gets a ton of points for this"

"So, does a winner in this competition level get awarded anything?" Kyle wanted to know.

"Yeah, the player with the highest score on the leader board will get a Gaming gift card that can, again, be redeemed for digital products or games."

"Wow."

"Indeed," Jeff sighed, "Project High had some studies on people selling menthol cigarettes in the inner city. You know how popular menthol cigarettes were with folks from that demographic before they were banned by the authorities, so the ability to be able to participate in a virtual game that is going to be so true to life in terms of visuals, AI agents, and so forth, will be transformative, and from what I hear we are sure to beat some competition out of the market." He looked pleased. "HH endorsed it wholeheartedly, so we are going forward with it."

"What can I say?" Kyle took a last sip of his coffee. "Let the games begin. I'm all for it though I'm sure some folks around here are likely opposed to it."

"Yup. Folks like Heather. I can already hear them saying 'How can we release a game that's so problematic in its treatment of minorities, women, underage kids, sexuality, and violence? Doesn't this violate diversity, equity, and inclusion related policies on some level or the spirit of these?'" Jeff shrugged. "When there is a market for something, I don't know who would be able to raise a business justification for those diversity, equity, and inclusion placard-carrying folks, do you? I have been sending that message to our DE&I champion." He rolled his eyes as if he had been on a long drawn-out battle with DE&I. "She has been such a big bother. She wants to augment the Online Code of Conduct to protect gamers based on race, gender, and blah, blah, blah. That's crazy, though, and she's crazy. Thankfully, Fiona is aligned with me."

"Atta girl," Kyle said.

"Yeah, Fiona's such a great team player! She gets that we shouldn't be fixing anything that ain't broke." Jeff continued, "See, if we're still making money and lots of it, the system ain't broke, right?"

"I tend to agree," Kyle nodded. "But how did the senior management team react when HH presented Project High?"

"HH didn't present it alone. The Innovation Incubation committee was there to co-present with him. We needed to get all our ducks in a row so that HH could announce it to everyone." Jeff grinned. "Let's just say that all directors had some high fives except for Ken Agrawal who tends to share Heather's sentiments, but no one paid any attention to him. This is a genius innovation, after all. We have the market, and we are even going to offer heavy discounts, knowing that folks from a certain demographic will get addicted to this kind of thing, and we will recoup our costs in the long run, for sure. Plus, it is a prime opportunity to collect those facial image datasets."

"Ah yes, like we said earlier, when John was here ..." Kyle left the words hanging.

"People-of-color-related datasets." Jeff folded his arms, leaning further into the desk. "It is going to aid our facial recognition and emotions tracking technology goals. This is nothing but a win-win all the way through."

Kyle let out a breath. "I can't wait to be in on all the launch-related work on this."

Jeff got up from his repose against the desk. "That's the main thing I needed to align with you. Let's make sure we have the right people from our team, all right? Especially the meetings. That's crucial."

"Jeff, leave it with me. I've got this handled."

Chapter Nine

"I really ought to get a date on this LTRc app, Jane, because, color me envious, is that your date parked outside our lawn in a Land Rover V8 SWB?" Leanne was peeking out at the front curb through the navy blue curtains that graced the windows of the living room.

"Leanne, get away from the window! You're embarrassing me!"

Leanne dropped the curtain as she watched Jane flick a hairbrush through her hair one last time and stuffed the portable brush into her black purse. "You look like you're going to the opera."

She referred, of course, to Jane's pencil skirt worn with a frilled black jersey shirt.

"Jealous much, roomie?"

"But I am," Leanne said without hesitation. "How long have you been chatting this one up on LTRc?"

"About three weeks."

"And you haven't dated anyone else since you last met with the Asian guy?"

"Stop calling him that. He has a name. And yes."

"How come he gets to pick you up from home? You didn't allow Mr. 'he has a name' to come here."

"Turns out that this guy and I have a mutual acquaintance from Harvard," Jane explained as her heels clicked on her way to the front door. We talked about our friend quite a bit on our online chats, and I checked him out with Faizel, my Harvard friend."

"Ah. A little dating investigation," Leanne stated. "I approve, as always. Don't miss curfew, my dear child."

"Yes, mother," Jane mocked good naturedly as she opened the front door and headed out toward the Land Rover parked at the curb.

****

Vikram Khatri climbed out of his white Land Rover as she approached. He walked around to the passenger side and pulled the door open for her with a smile.

"Vikram," Jane said rather formally, stopping for a moment to smile at him as he held the door open. He stood a head taller than she. And he was definitely fairer than brown. In fact, she secretly wondered if she could ask him if he used any particular skin products! You probably should not ask a guy that though. Especially on a first date.

"Jane. You look very beautiful."

She ducked her head with a sudden onslaught of self-consciousness and cleared her throat, "Um.

Thanks." She hurriedly got into the passenger seat. Vikram closed the door behind her and went around back to the driver's side.

He pulled the car out onto the street.

"You look so young!" she blurted out and almost bit her tongue.

He laughed, "Thanks, I think. My pictures on LTRc don't do me justice?

She shook her head.

"I could say the same for you. You have a certain Beyoncé look. I know it sounds corny."

"You are right. It does!" she giggled. "Now I'm curious to know what you would say next when I finally tell you what I do for a living."

"There is that! I could not get our friend, Faizel, to reveal anything. You must have him on a tight leash."

Faizel Ismail was a friend of Jane's from undergrad school. He had gone on to become an engineer at a big firm in Chicago.

"Where are you taking me?"

"Don't you worry about a thing. Sit back and relax, and let me create a really good night for us, eh?"

She felt a sense of ease and sat back in the seat, watching him as he continued to drive, barely noticing as the Land Rover pulled into the parking lot of an Indian restaurant, Saffron Grill, on North Northgate Way.

He got out again and opened the door for her.

"I could get used to this," Jane commented as she glanced around at the building. "I've never been here."

"You will love this place. Come," and he proceeded to tuck her hand under his arm and led the way into the restaurant.

There was a tall, beautiful lady wearing a pink *sari* right at the entrance. She bowed with a smile and gestured them towards the seating area. Jane was not sure if she was the maître d' or possibly even the owner. She had never seen the maître d' at any Indian restaurant she had been to wearing a sari before. Maybe she was just in for a special treat tonight, and this was not always the case. She was, after all, feeling quite special already.

Vikram was a perfect gentleman. She stole a glance at him as he settled in the seat across the table from her.

She had already asked copious questions during their interactions on the LTRc app. He was a mechanical engineer and worked for a big Seattle engineering firm. He was a second generation American. His parents had been born and bred in the United States.

Jane never asked the question, so maybe he was not in the market for an arranged marriage from his family. She wondered about it more than once since they started chatting.

"So are you in the market for an arranged marriage with your family?" The very question that Jane had in her head spilled off her tongue, word-for-word. *Jane. Jane. Jane. When will you tame your tongue?*

Vikram's face, perfectly symmetrical in her view, with the broad forehead and amazingly smooth skin tone, looked slightly surprised. "Arranged marriage? What, you believe all the stereotypes, too?"

Jane's hand was covering her mouth. "I'm sorry! I just ... Okay, go ahead, ask me."

He looked like he was trying hard not to laugh, "Ask you what?"

"Is my favorite music rap music?" she asked the question herself.

"Ah, yes. The ever-present Black stereotype. A Black person is drawn only to rap music or rhythm and blues."

"True to an extent," Jane sighed. "But I would deserve it if you believed that of me."

"Well, I think rhythm and blues is lovely music, and you have a right to love whatever sound preference you desire."

She smiled, "Goodness. Thanks, Vikram. But I had to ask that question earlier."

"Okay, here goes." He looked ready for a hurricane to hit him, but he was smiling. He clasped both hands in tent-like fashion on the table and gave her a studious look before speaking, "You were right to speak up about my culture and arranged marriages. It is common in India. But my family is ... progressive.

My older brother is married to a White woman and my younger brother is dating a Pacific Islander."

"Quite an adventurous bunch you guys are."

"Compatibility is not dependent on race," he said punctuating the word race in air quotes with his fingers. "It is a function of acceptance. Not that folks who date within their races are not accepting human beings."

"I know what you mean on both counts, Vikram. Race is definitely a social construct; we're all part of one human race. And yes, I couldn't agree with you more on that acceptance piece." She was feeling warm and at home in this restaurant with this cute guy.

"May I take your order?" A waiter was standing at their table before she knew it.

Vikram gestured with a hand, "Allow me." He picked up the menu and read out the offerings. "May I interest the lady in a curry special made with beef, served with sautéed vegetables and a side of samosas? And I will have the royal biryani with paneer."

Jane stared.

The waiter took the menu, smiled, and hurried off.

Vikram gave Jane a triumphant look, "You are going to love it. I promise."

****

It was delicious. And she couldn't get over it. He had ordered dinner for her.

"Do you do that all the time?" she wondered as she chewed at the last samosa.

"Do what?"

"Order dinner for everyone?"

"Only for the lady I consider special, which is rare."

She almost melted but didn't. "Oh, special." Why was the word not doing its usual magic to her psyche tonight? She liked special.

"How is everything?" the waiter was back with a smile.

"Awesome. Why didn't we get the wet towels yet? I thought I asked for some like ten minutes ago? The lady needs to wipe her fingers, right? Greasy samosas and all?"

"Yes sir," the waiter replied as he hurried away.

Vikram shook his head. "It's not like they're busy tonight. Some waitstaff just need to pay more attention to their customers."

Jane sipped her iced tea. "Sounds as if you've had bad experiences with waitstaff."

"Just incompetent ones, that's all."

"Have you ever waited tables, Vikram?"

He laughed, "Why would I need to wait tables?"

She sipped her tea again. The waiter was back with the wet towels. Jane smiled her thanks and took one.

"Are you planning to refill the iced tea pitcher?" Vikram asked the waiter with a cool smile.

The waiter hurried away to get a fresh pitcher.

****

The white Land Rover sat idling on the curb at Jane's house.

"So? What did you think of dinner?" Vikram stretched an arm to the back of her chair.

"Delicious."

"Yeah. I told you."

"Yes. You did, Vikram."

"We should do this again."

Jane reached for the passenger door. Seeing her movement. Vikram jumped out, ran to her side of the car, and pulled it open for her.

"You are such a gentleman, Vikram." She smiled at him; he smiled back.

Jane said, "I used to wait tables to pay rent in college."

"Yeah?" he said, still smiling.

Clearly, he did not get it.

"I'm beat. Goodnight, Vikram."

And she left him on the curb without a hug, without a backward glance.

****

Tiffany Johnson started typing into the Gaming instant messaging system for the umpteenth time. Then quickly deleted her half-written message.

The name of the intended recipient was at the top of the instant message box.

Jane Jackson, Recruitment and HR, HR Generalist.

She had typed, erased, and re-typed the same message for the past fifteen minutes.

Around her, Monday morning was awakening. The legal floor was rapidly filling up with legal assistants, paralegals, and junior associates. The seniors would arrive later, as few came in before 8 a.m.

Tiffany typed.

Gaming Instant Messenger

Tiffany Johnson (Legal Counsel):

Jane, we've met once. I've been an associate with legal for the past three years. I need to talk to you.

She hit send. A message popped up in less than a minute. Jane Jackson.

Jane Jackson (HR Generalist):

Tiffany. Hi! Of course, let's talk. Do you want me to call you?

Tiffany Jackson (Legal Counsel):

No, I'm in the open office area. Probably best if we message for now.

Jane Jackson (HR Generalist):

What's on your mind Tiffany?

Tiffany Johnson (Legal Counsel):

Have you ever heard of game AI agents that need to be designed to mimic an angry Black "hood rat" character?

Instant message went silent. Jane Jackson was probably sitting uncertainly at her desk wondering what to say to that and where this was going.

Tiffany typed again.

Tiffany Johnson (Legal Counsel):

Exactly. Shocks the conscience, doesn't it? Welcome to my world. The lone Black girl in legal gets to hear all the dark secrets of what non-Blacks think about us.

Jane Jackson (HR Generalist):

I don't know what to say ... write. Someone said that to you?

Tiffany Johnson (Legal Counsel):

Not yet. But I overhead them. Kyle, Jeff, and John talking about how aggressive and angry I come across and, essentially, how much of a "hood rat" I am.

Silence again. Jane was no longer typing back. Tiffany picked up the conversation again.

Tiffany Johnson (Legal Counsel):

Maybe this is a conversation we should be having face-to-face.

Jane Jackson (HR Generalist):

I would like that. Here's my cell phone number so we can arrange.

****

Jane sat back in her chair and blew out her breath, still unbelieving. What on Earth was that about? More accurately, was Tiffany making it up? A lawyer with a good head on her shoulders if she had managed to snag a job at Gaming was clearly not cuckoo or trying to make baseless accusations. She would know better than that.

She could not get the picture out of her mind. A C-suite person like Jeff had been involved in that kind of conversation? Jane knew she now had questions about Kyle and maybe would not be too surprised if she began to hear unnerving things about him.

After all, his own manager had been calling him a "pass off" in the cafeteria with his friend only a few weeks ago. Kyle already had a question mark in her mind about his person.

But Jeff? C-suite Jeff Erikson? One of the folks she had come to look up to as upstanding through her short life at Gaming already? If those comments Tiffany heard were true, they were unacceptable.

Jane looked around and spotted her manager, Tracey, sitting in her office, hanging up the phone after a phone call.

Tracey was available. Jane had to tell this to someone higher to help her handle. She got up from her desk and walked towards Tracey's office.

Chapter Ten

"Got a minute, Tracey?" Jane stood at the entrance to Tracey's office.

"Of course. Come on in, Jane."

Jane walked in and closed the door.

"Please, sit! What's on your mind?" Tracey was clearly in a good mood.

Jane sat, "How is the hiring going for legal?"

"As planned," Tracey beamed. "Jag Kumar started work this week. And we already have the next candidate lined up. She will be receiving a call later today with the offer."

"Oh? Who are we hiring?"

"Her name is Carla Thunderhawk." Tracey smiled. "Native."

Jane did not smile back, "Quite a diverse group that we're getting in legal."

"Isn't it?" Tracey looked pleased.

"Tracey, I know this isn't our remit here at Gaming, but are we delivering training on our DE&I policies? Okay, I'm sure we are but are we really hammering the lessons home? Also, is anyone looking into whether there's any bias embedded in video game products or services we're looking to launch?"

Tracey was no longer smiling. "What do you mean, Jane?"

Jane felt her heart start to race. Okay, her palms had broken out in that nerve-induced sweat. She could not rub them on her thighs to clean them up. It would give her away, how she was fighting to bring this point up. How could she put this?

"Someone overheard a conversation," Jane decided simply to blurt it out. "It was about the new AI and virtual reality strategy that Gaming is embarking upon. It seems there are some employees who think it's appropriate to make discriminatory statements about females of color." Jane stopped talking.

Tracey was looking at her with a poker face. That mask that managers wore so that you did not know what they were thinking? Yes, that one.

"And who did you overhear saying this?"

Jane shook her head, "Someone overheard."

"Does the 'someone' have a name?"

Jane sighed and let the cat out of the bag: "Tiffany Johnson in legal."

There was a strange look on Tracey's face. It was quickly gone before Jane had a chance to decipher it. "And who did Tiffany overhear? Did she tell you?"

Tracey's features were unreadable. Jane sat straight and stiffly in her seat, unsure of the next words to say. Her gut felt tight with the effort of trying to look unflustered, but she could feel her heart rate picking up with nerves.

Why did she have a bad feeling about this conversation?

"Some of her colleagues," she said evasively.

"Jane. I don't think you heard my question: Did she tell you *who* they were?"

She was asking because there would be retribution. That had to be it. The "boys" in legal had something coming. Relax Jane.

"It was Jeff, Kyle, and John," Jane said at last.

Tracey's facial expression did not twitch or move in any direction, be it surprise or acknowledgment of what Jane just said. Nothing.

"Was she lodging an official complaint when she spoke to you? Think about that question very carefully, Jane," Tracey asked.

"Um, now that I think of it, she actually did not use that particular language."

"That will be all, Jane. You can go back to your desk."

Jane almost didn't move for an entire ten seconds.

Tracey's askance stare made her jump to her feet, "Um. Okay. Thank you, Tracey."

And Jane fled to her desk, feeling like a child who had just been reprimanded even though, technically, Tracey had not said a word.

****

John was knocking on Kyle's office door by 10 a.m. sharp on Wednesday morning. He would have come knocking earlier; however, Kyle had just walked in for the day. Better to snag his attention before it got snagged by all the other "droids" on the floor of the legal department.

"Kyle," he knocked softly on the door, "may I come in?"

Kyle gestured enthusiastically that he should as he spoke into the receiver of his desk phone. "Yeah, got it, Jack. All right. Thanks." he hung up. "Mind shutting my door?"

John turned around quickly to do as ordered, then turned back to look at his manager as he gingerly sat across from Kyle's seat at the office desk. "Got your voice message last night," John looked apologetic. "I didn't see it until later, or I would have called back sooner. I was at dinner ..."

"Well, John, next time, I recommend that you excuse yourself from dinner and take my calls."

John looked put down. "Sorry."

"Hey! I'm just messing with you!" Kyle laughed, "We all gotta eat. So the reason I was calling was to update you on the conversation we had yesterday with the BD team. There's a lot coming down the pike around this new virtual reality project, John."

As he repeated exactly what Jeff had revealed to him the night before about Project High, the new virtual reality game coming soon, John's eyes widened with each revelation.

"All I can say is. 'Wow," John gushed. "I mean, really?"

"John, all *I* can say is, the meetings and execution-related work from this will be brutal and we will have to be on our toes. So young recruit, I hereby knight you as my *Obi Wan Kenobi*. You are going to be my help and right-hand man through all this as soon as you're disclosed. Alright?"

John looked as pale as a sheet.

"Hey? Something wrong?" Kyle wanted to know.

"You will not be attending meetings?"

"Not always. I have other projects. Would this be a problem for you?"

John quickly shook his head, "Of course not. I'm on it. Will I have the meeting invitations forwarded to me, then? I haven't heard or received anything since yesterday."

"Don't you worry about that. I'll take care of all meeting notifications and will have the guy managing the NDAs reach out to you so we can get that squared off. Well, Putin, looks like you and I are going to be up for some amazing adventures together."

John looked like he had shrunk a size or two in his chair, "Yeah."

"Speaking of adventures, I have a trip planned for Luxembourg in a week. You will be coming with me. It's going to be one of those Legal-Incubation

Innovation type show-downs with our international team."

John looked surprised. "Lux? Okay! I thought a lot of international meetings are now being held over video conferencing in line with HH's general cost-saving outlook. Is there anything we need to demonstrate to them live that can't be done remotely?"

"We are going to Lux," Kyle said dismissively. "Jeff will sign off on our expense reimbursement claims. He's never looked into whether they are necessary or questioned the quantum of the claims. I highly doubt that he's going to start now."

There was a gentle knock on Kyle's office door. It opened slightly. They both turned to see Tracey standing in the doorway with a smile.

"Oops!" Tracey said apologetically. "I thought you were alone, Kyle. Someone told me out here that they believed you were."

"It's okay, Trace. John and I were just done."

John rose to his feet immediately and hurried out of the office.

Tracey walked in and firmly closed the door.

"Whenever you do that, Madam HR, I always feel like I'm about to get a reprimand from the school principal," Kyle sighed.

"Do what? Close the office door? Kyle, I'm HR. Everything I discuss with you is classified. Right?"

Kyle leaned forward in his seat, "All right. What privileged and confidential discussion are we holding today?"

Tracey sat in the chair John had just vacated.

It was obvious that she had done this often. The casual and relaxed air in the room spoke of many conversations that Tracey had held with Kyle about human resources.

"I got a buzz, Kyle," Tracey revealed.

Kyle expected an unpleasant blow. "Let me have it."

"It is my professional opinion that when you and the other guys from legal are having disparaging conversations about women and/or people of color, you may want to do it at a location where fellow employees may not hear the ripples from the talk."

Kyle's face was blank, "What are you talking about?"

"Tell me if this rings a bell: Tiffany is not a culture fit; she is a hood rat with a horrible accent and comes across as angry and scary."

Kyle's face remained blank. Tracey had to hand it to the guy. He would do well in courtroom litigation.

"You don't remember this conversation, Kyle?"

"I don't think I follow. Who is saying that I had it?"

"One of your own direct reports."

"Name?"

Tracey gave it up, "Tiffany Johnson. One of your associate counsels."

Kyle sat back in his chair, his face ominous, "I see."

"We will need some damage control."

"I'm not sure where Ms. Johnson got her ideas from."

"Kyle, Kyle, Kyle. Stop." Tracey was the one who looked slightly ominous. "Let me respectfully remind you that this is not the first time you and I have had conversations like this, and for that reason, I'm going to err on the side of caution and not argue about what was said or not said. Thankfully, she has not lodged an official compliant, or at least, that's the position we can take if this really goes south. If she does, she won't have any proof, it will be her word against yours. For now though, let's just focus on damage control. Is that okay with you?"

Kyle looked like a twelve-year-old sulking in his chair. He shrugged, "Whatever."

Tracey sat back in her chair, too, and looked at him like an older aunt considering her petulant nephew. "Kyle, you and I have had many conversations over the past three years since joining us. You are a Gamer now. You know the HR rules. My team and Heather's have to evolve policies around the activities that your team embarks upon. It is important that you remember that."

"Okay, so what evolution will you be developing with this latest accusation?" he wanted to know.

Tracey gave him a frank look. "We will have to embark on some diversity, equity, and inclusion campaigns. Make it obvious company wide and externally that we are diversity, equity, and inclusion champions. It is the pre-emptive strike against anyone who wishes to suggest that bias and discrimination is condoned within the company's walls. Right?"

He shrugged again. "You are the HR expert, Trace."

A thrill went down her spine. *Recognition.*

"So we have all four new associates hired as targeted for the legal team this month."

Kyle warmed up to the change in subject. "Yes. John, Carla, Jagadish, and Silvia. Tell me, Tracey, how can anyone say, *looking* at my new hires, that I don't have any regard for people of color or women and that we are not diversity and inclusion conscious?"

Tracey sighed inwardly and lifted up her fingers to count: "John is White, Carla is Native Indian, Jag is South Asian, and Sylvia is Latino. We did a good job on diversity recruitment. But that is not sufficient in the eyes of the world. We are supposed to do more."

"What more? Like, add a new Black hire to the mix?" Kyle asked, irritated.

Tracey kept her mouth shut, but of course her head ran through the facts. Yes, the four new hires had just come on board. Yet even though she was only the HR rep who should have no business in, well, a department's operations, she was well aware of the fact that the new hires did not have much work to go around between them.

She knew HR and Legal had approved the hiring, but the approval was way beyond her pay grade. She only did what she was told. And that was to hire four new lawyers for the legal department who would report to Kyle. What they were actually meant to do was not within her purview. She silently wished they could engineer the promotion of one of them shortly to direct attention from this Tiffany *caca*, but she knew it was too soon to play that card. They were far too new, too inexperienced, and they didn't even have any substantive work to speak of to begin with. But maybe she needed to talk to Heather and Fiona about getting HH's buy-in on hiring more senior people of color into various departments across the company. That might help. *Shit*. This was such a mess.

"Okay, here's an idea," Tracey suddenly piped up. "Martin Luther King Day is coming up soon. I think it would be really great if you could share something about MLK and say something about how important it is that we continue to advocate for a more just, equitable, and inclusive America. What do you think? Can you put something together or should I ask one of Heather's folks to draft something for you?"

Kyle wasn't really sure what to say about this. It didn't really sound like he had a choice in the matter. "Hmm, okay. I ...," his voice faltered, "I guess I could do that. I can put something together."

"Great!" Tracey interjected, and, when it suddenly hit her that Kyle's write-up could contain some hair raising *faux pas*, she quickly added, "You know, let me ask one of Heather's senior managers to put something together for you and send it over - all you'll have to do is hit 'send' so you can be free to attend to your important work. Why don't we do that?"

"Okay, thanks, Trace."

"So keeping the new kids busy?" Tracey changed the subject as she sat on the edge of her seat, a move indicating she was ready to end this visit.

A soft knock sounded on Kyle's door. Tracey turned around to see a dark-haired, slender Silvia Lopez, one of the new counsel hires from three months ago. Tracey still could not get over how strikingly beautiful Silvia was.

"Sorry," she spoke in an uncertain, shy voice, her eyes darting to Kyle and then to Tracey seated across his desk. "I will come back..."

"As you can see, I do keep my counsel busy," Kyle remarked in Tracey's direction triumphantly. Then he called out, "Silvia, come on in. Let's get busy here, shall we?"

Tracey got up from her chair and walked towards the door as Silvia literally snuck past her to get in, as if trying to make herself look smaller and unnoticeable. Tracey had noted the rather bashful personality of the young counsel, right from day one of her hire. Apparently, she had not quite opened up yet.

"I'll keep you posted, Kyle!" Tracey called back to him and exited the office.

****

Silvia came out of Kyle's office, running her fingers through her frazzled hair. She was hugging the laptop she had taken in with her as she made her way back to her desk.

Tiffany thought the posture was quite strange, like a little girl trying to protect herself from something, unsure of herself or, at the least, trying to make herself as small and unnoticeable as possible. She had always thought Silvia was a beautiful mouse. No insult intended. Mouse, as in she was so quiet and seemed always to like remaining invisible. She sat across from Tiffany and Sarah, and they had often gone for coffee together.

As Silvia sat, Tiffany offered, "Coffee?"

There was a look of absolute appreciation on Silvia's face. "Please."

They each grabbed their wallets and headed for the elevator.

Ten minutes and two Starbucks lattes later, they were strolling back towards the Venus building. "So do I start with my troubles, or should I give you first choice?" Tiffany wanted to know.

"Tiffany, I think I can confidently say my troubles do not add up to yours," Silvia declared, looking down at her latte cup as if she were studying the steam that rose from it.

"I don't know about that. You've never told me any real problems before, and I know you're not immune. You just seem to handle things so well."

Silvia sighed, "I don't know about that. I was given your third-party game developer contract project, and I couldn't help but wonder, okay, what does this mean?"

Tiffany shrugged, trying to look nonchalant but knowing that it made her belly hurt. What did it mean indeed? Another lawyer had been given the one high visibility project she had. Was she on her way out the door of Gaming? Were they getting rid of her?

"I think I'm being retaliated against, Silvia," Tiffany confessed.

Silvia looked at her sharply, "It sounds like something illegal is afoot. Why do you say that?"

"How long have we known each other? Three months since you joined Gaming?"

"Yes. And without your buddy-ship and support, I don't know how I would have made it this far, Tiffany."

"Ah. Don't mention it. My three-year-old Gaming experience is golden."

"You make me nervous when you talk about retaliation. As if your three-year tenure is suddenly going to be, 'Poof!'" Silvia exclaimed.

"I definitely think my career's in jeopardy. I said something to HR. I know that it's unlawful under the Washington Law against Discrimination for an employer to retaliate against a person for reporting what the person reasonably believed to be discrimination on the basis of race and gender and that Gaming's conduct constitutes adverse employment action against me, but it's potentially going to take a lot of time, money, and a great attorney to fend this off and successfully assert my rights."

Silvia was mesmerized. "What did you say?"

Tiffany paused. What did she have to lose in telling a fellow colleague? Her projects were being reassigned. It was clearly not a big secret among the senior managers, so she opened her mouth and started talking.

****

One hour flew by like a breeze. Jane had barely just left the office to take a quick drive to the nearby shopping center to pick up a pair of green shoes. Yes, she had yet to buy that color in her shoe's ensemble. She knew it was going to go perfectly with her dress for the date she had tonight.

A third date in the last six weeks. No repeats so far. What was she becoming, a serial dater?

Armed with her shopping bag, she drove quickly back towards the Gaming office building, her eye on the time. She had a 1:30 meeting with Tracey. It was a mystery what the agenda was about. She thought meetings were supposed to come with those. Anyway, Tracey was the boss. She could call meetings as she wished. Right?

As she pulled into a mercifully available parking spot, Jane's phone buzzed on the passenger seat. Frowning, she grabbed it as she turned off the car. The number was a local area code, and it looked familiar.

"Hello?"

"Jane?"

She certainly recognized the deep, somber voice. A voice from the past.

"Duke?" Her first LTRc date—Duke?

"Hey," he sounded somewhat hesitant. "I suppose you lost my number."

Jane got out of the car, picking up her new shoes and went to stash them in the rear. "Something like that. It's been, what? Several months since we last saw each other"

"Ouch."

So many months after their date and he was calling her? Like he still had her number?

Okay. So maybe that was cruel. But the memory of that date night was still fresh in her mind, and it burned. "I figured you would prefer hanging out with your friends. Why are you calling me?" she demanded, trotting towards the office building.

"Jane, look, I didn't mean to ..."

Jane's phone buzzed. The caller ID flashed Tiffany Johnson's name.

"I gotta go," and she hung up on him. Her heart raced. She was not sure if it was because an old date had just called her and she wanted nothing to do with him or that Tiffany was calling her, and she kind of knew what was coming next.

"Hi Tiffany," Jane said as jovially as she could.

"Jane. It's getting weird up here."

Jane lowered her voice as she stopped short just at the entrance of the Gaming building, "What's going on, Tiffany?"

"I should probably be asking you," Tiffany said, in what could only be a whisper. She was most likely in the Gaming building somewhere, trying to keep the exchange as quiet as possible. "Any thoughts about what we talked about?"

Jane felt her tummy dip. "Tiffany, we're both lawyers, so I expect my advice is likely not going to be anything you haven't already considered, but I'll share it anyway. Confidentially, I suggest you consider filing a formal complaint internally and that you also reach out to an attorney.

"I would also recommend if there's anyone you trust on the BGN, that you canvass their opinion as well. Perhaps you can even work with them to address these issues corporately as it looks like there are systemic issues at work here." Jane took a deep breath, wondering if she had just spoken words that betrayed her profession as HR. "That's all I can say."

A momentary silence ensued. Jane was not sure what the other woman was thinking. Had she said the right words that Tiffany needed to hear? Had she insulted her as Tiffany could feel she was being blown off?

Jane held her breath as Tiffany exhaled slowly, reminding Jane of that movie with Whitney Houston. This was such a moment. Just, let it out. She hoped Tiffany would be frank with her.

"You are right," Tiffany said at last. "I have considered all that, but I find myself in such a catch-22 situation. If I file a complaint, I can practically kiss my career goodbye." Jane kept her mouth shut because yes, she knew that Tiffany would be as good as fired.

"The company will initiate an investigation, but I highly doubt that Jeff and John will confirm my side of the story." Tiffany continued, "So in the end, Kyle will be exonerated, and he will retaliate in one way or another against me. I can't see how Gaming will be able to protect me. I'll likely have to end up leaving. Kyle will likely also spread his views of my performance in the market, so I may struggle to find comparable employment in the city."

"A lot of conjecture," Jane tried to play devil's advocate.

"You know I'm right," Tiffany said firmly.

Jane fell silent again.

"If I don't file a complaint," Tiffany continued, "Kyle will just keep making my work environment untenable in some way. He'll likely also continue rating my performance badly so that I'm put on a change management program, so in the end, I may just be forced to leave Gaming."

This time around, Jane was wise enough simply to listen without comment.

"So, it just looks like a lose-lose situation. I've been trying to see if there's an alternate winning scenario, but I'm coming up short so far. I've considered trying to find another team that I could transfer to here at Gaming but I highly doubt Kyle will support me on that. I guess, I can leave the company right now but that's not really a winning scenario. Not the kind of winning scenario I deserve. Perhaps a visit to an attorney's office may help, as you suggest. Let me seriously consider that."

Jane felt it was an opportunity to say an encouraging word now to propel her in the right direction, for what it was worth. "Please do," she said quietly.

Tiffany was silent for almost half a minute. "Well, you've given more advice than other professionals I've had the opportunity of interacting with in my experience with diversity, equity, and *including* us."

"I'm sorry, Tiffany," Jane was not sure on whose behalf she was apologizing, but she felt she had to. "I have to go and get prepped for a meeting with my manager. Talk again soon?"

"Coincidence—I have a meeting with my own manager in a few minutes too. Break a leg."

Jane laughed nervously and hung up.

The invisibility blanket had fallen on her again.

She hurried toward the elevator.

Chapter Eleven

"How is your day going, Tiffany?" Kyle greeted her warmly as his direct report, associate counsel, Tiffany, walked into the office.

Tiffany sat in the chair opposite from Kyle in his office.

"Peachy," she could not stop the word from coming out of her mouth. It hung in the air.

Kyle's smile was chevalier bright. It made Tiffany's spine stiffen. "So we're at that time of the year. Time when we need to review if we're demonstrating competency in the basic requirements of our legal functions at the level we're pegged at. Yay."

Tiffany tried to keep the frown off her face.

There had been emails from Kyle over the past month that such-and-such analysis that she had provided was lacking "robustness," or that some other memo she had composed was not written well enough for the argument they were trying to pursue, or how there were complaints, but never any evidence to substantiate this, that any BD email requests for support from her on one-off queries had disappeared into a black hole and had not been addressed. A black hole. She couldn't believe her eyes when she saw that one. Kyle, doling out a pejorative double entendres without so much as a second thought.

But Tiffany had not changed her writing, research style, or responsiveness rate in the three years of being here. How had these suddenly become a problem in a month's time span? Maybe this conversation should be about her compensation, assertiveness, and angry Black hood rat nature.

"I don't know how, in the last two or more meetings that we've had about my tasks, we've never really talked about how I'm aware of a conversation that involved derogatory statements made against a particular group of people."

"Oh?"

How could his expression be so cluelessly surprised? Tiffany had intended to shock him by springing up the subject unannounced. After all, what direct report had the nerve to confront their manager about topics like that? And Kyle sat looking shocked. How the ...? How could he manage such acting?

"Angry Black women. Hood rats. Scary." Tiffany said the three phrases. She had been known to be a drama queen, even back in college. She had been in a few plays and shows before she decided to switch from theater to political science and then to law—long story. So she could be dramatic.

"I don't know what you are talking about, Tiffany."

She inwardly seethed. *Oh, no, Mr. Smith. Was this how it was going down?*

"That I spoke to HR about a conversation involving my 'aggressiveness,' accent, and Black people, women in particular, from the hood?" she asked casually. "Someone, I don't recall names, said the topic had been raised with management. They promised to keep my manager in the loop with the assurance that Gaming is an organization that is very conscientious about employee well-being and dealing with said concerns judiciously."

A muscle seemed to jump on Kyle's cheek as if he was trying to keep a rein on something, "I did hear about that, and didn't think much of it. Being a *free* society, everyone is *free* to interpret the things they hear as they see fit, in the same way that everyone else is *free* to talk about whatever it is that they deem fit."

Blah-blah-blah. If he said the word *free* one more time, she was sure it would hit a record sufficient for a lotto win.

This time, Tiffany's mouth did drop open, "Fit? Okay, may I ask, how should I respond, as a Black person, to someone who says I'm not fit for corporate culture because of my skin tone, gender, accent, schooling, and where I grew up?"

"That's the way you see it. Unfortunately, it is not the way I do."

She sat, frustrated. Okay. She would approach via another angle.

"Kyle, I don't know what's going on, but I have questions. The only project that I had been reviewing over the last two weeks has been pulled and given to Silvia. I'm no longer managing the game developer contracts for some reason. My workload seems to entail only the document reviews of mini projects."

She stopped talking. The triumphant look on Kyle's face was only momentary but wiped away quickly before it lingered. "Are you asking me a question, Tiffany?"

"Yes, I'd like to understand what is going on," she asked point-blank.

A look of shock was plastered on his face. "Tiffany, when serious questions arise at Gaming with regards to performance, we always give our employees options before making any final decisions."

She stared, flabbergasted, "Oh. We are back to *performance*?"

He looked confused. No, he feigned the look very well, "Is that not why I called this meeting? Is it not that time of the year?"

She gave up. Tiffany fell silent and listened to another five minutes of Kyle droning on about her areas of strength, opportunity for improvement, and her stretch performance. The words that came at the tail end shook her to alertness again.

"In situations like this, poor performers are given two options under the Change Program—leaving the company with severance or starting a performance improvement plan under enhanced management review."

Tiffany could feel the boiling heat emanating from her ears. "I'm being placed *on a Change Program?*"

He looked perfectly innocent. "Only if you want to. Like I mentioned ..."

"I could choose severance," she interrupted what he was about to say.

He nodded. "That's exactly right."

She knew that the PIP route wasn't an option for her. Kyle, as her manager, would need to rate her fairly and that was never, in a million years, going to happen. She felt defeated. She didn't know what to say.

All this because she raised legitimate concerns about being discriminated against and, rather than address those concerns, Gaming was effectively firing her?

"Can I go ... think? I would like to go back to my desk, please." She knew she sounded like a little girl. She didn't know how else to respond. She needed to get out of here.

"Tiffany, of course. You have 48 hours to think about it. HR will ping you with all the pertinent details outlining your performance issues, whom you can contact if you have any questions relating to your options, by when you need to respond, and to whom. In the meantime, is there anything you need me to do for you?"

"Um, no?"

"Okay, so as I said, don't worry about getting back to me on anything right now. Take the time to reflect."

Tiffany hurried out of the office, feeling too humiliated to look at her manager's face as she left, failing to look up at the two men who were just about to walk into Kyle's office.

****

Jeff shook his head mentally as he watched Tiffany rush past Scot van Berg, Director of Legal, and him as they walked and spoke quietly on their way into Kyle's office.

"She looked rushed," Scot observed needlessly, looking after the rushing female.

Jeff glanced at Tiffany's profile. Now, why did he think he knew what *that* was about? He knocked on Kyle's office door, "Hey, Kyle, got a minute?"

Kyle rose up from his desk at the sight of his manager. "Hi. Jeff. Scot! Come on in!"

Both men walked in, and Jeff gently closed the door behind him. "Everything okay?" He didn't need to mention Tiffany's name.

"All good." Kyle spread out his arms in a charismatic way. "I love visitors."

"I should stop by more often, then," Scot joked. "I feel as if I haven't seen you in a long time. How are you doing these days, Kyle?"

"Always perfect. Always perfect, Scot."

"Kyle, I only have a few minutes before my next call. Thought I would get you both formally connected today." Jeff jumped right to the point in a smooth tone. "I was just speaking with Scot earlier today about some updates we're having to management structure."

"Oh?" Kyle said cautiously.

"Kyle, Scot is going to be the line manager for you and your team, effective immediately. I'll shoot an update email off to our team and the BD folks shortly. I will still make myself available, of course, for any projects involving the BD veep or any pressing escalations. However, I'm sure you and Scot will be able to manage things well between you."

Scot was all smiles. "I'm sure we will."

Kyle cleared his throat. "This is great. Awesome. Okay, we have a new reporting line structure. Change is good!"

"Excellent," said Jeff, already heading for the door. "I'll leave you two alone so you can get better acquainted with each other."

Ten minutes later, Jeff's phone pinged as he sat on his conference call in his office.

Gaming Instant Messenger

Kyle Smith (Senior Legal Counsel):

Jeff. Are we okay?

Jeff hid a smile to himself. The tantrum. He had expected it. Clearly, Kyle had the features of a young child when he was uncertain about himself. Getting a new boss unannounced was a shocking thing, true. Most people took it in their stride. Kyle didn't have that kind of self-esteem. Jeff knew.

He messaged back.

Jeff Erikson (VP, Legal):

Nothing to worry about, Kyle. Just minor structural updates.

****

"Jane. Do you have a minute to come into my office?" Tracey asked.

"Of course."

Jane went into her manager's office and closed the door.

"How are you feeling since our last talk?"

Jane sat still in her chair. What was this? A check in?

What was their last talk about again? Oh yes, Tiffany overhearing some talk.

"I'm good," she announced.

"Glad to hear it." Check-in done. Tracey appeared ready to go to the point: "We need to start a radical DE&I campaign."

Jane's face blanked. "A what now?"

"I need you to spearhead a diversity, equity, and inclusion campaign with the DE&I team, which will demonstrate internally and externally that leadership opposes discrimination and values diversity in all its forms." Tracey drilled out the orders in one breath. "I'm sure Heather's team will have ideas of their own on this, but I want us to recommend that every department head come up with a five-year DE&I plan for its team and put together a committee comprised of employees and leadership that will work on team specific initiatives, a two-hour training program for all employees, and the recruitment of minority senior management and executives." At last, she paused to take a breath; then launched onwards again: "Information on every department activity and accomplishment must be regularly shared with employees in that department."

Radical. Plus, campaign. Two disturbing words mixed with diversity, equity, and inclusion in the context of what Jane had come to know about the legal team.

Jane was learning new terminology. She knew what to call this radical campaign. Another management protection program. It's not about the employees; it's about serving management. What had Tracey's exact words intimated at their first meeting when Jane left the room, confused about her job duties? Yes, HR was the management protection bureau. Protection from violations of employees' rights and dignity. Jane felt something right in the pit of her stomach. It was rising like bile to her throat.

"But why do we in HR need to get involved in this campaign? More specifically, why me?"

Tracey had her mouth open, about to say a few more things about her campaign plans. Jane's words appeared to have stumped her. She shut her mouth and considered Jane quizzically for a moment. As if the question had hit her unexpectedly.

"Why you?" Tracey repeated Jane's question, as if she had not heard it the first time.

Jane shrugged, injecting innocence and cluelessness into her gesture, "Yeah?"

"Oh, but it's obvious," Tracey raised her hand palm up. "We are one team! One for the team! We work together to create a cohesive environment, since we fall under Fiona's remit. Our approach to HR and DE&I must be taken as a holistic whole."

"I don't understand. Shouldn't DE&I have its own champion for 'wholeness' campaigns so we can focus on managing employee recruitment and termination and the like?"

"So who will support DE&I if not us?" Tracey looked as if she were getting impatient.

"Someone from Heather's team ...?" Jane began.

"She doesn't have anyone suitable, anyone, how shall I say, of the right hue on her team," Tracey blurted out.

Silence. Oh. That was it.

Tracey's face looked red. "Besides, weren't you asking me about DE&I-related training just a short while ago?" she quickly added.

Jane figured she would spare her the torture.

"I would be happy to get going on a diversity, equity, and inclusion campaign, Tracey," Jane said, all smiles.

****

"Third date in six weeks?"

"I got the shoes to celebrate it." Jane brandished her new green shoes, still safely in their box as she hurried towards her room to get dressed.

"So who is the lucky guy from LTRc this time?" Leanne called out from the living room.

"I will let you guess. While you're guessing," Jane added to her roommate, "I suggest you consider using the dating app yourself. This is getting really creepy that every time I have a date, you are always home, interrogating me about it!"

"It speaks to my lack of a life, roomie!" Leanne lamented from the living room.

"That's my point exactly. Get on the app, girl!"
Jane shouted back.

Her phone, lying on her bed, rang. Jane
jumped to grab it. She knew it wasn't her date. He
didn't have her number yet. She was planning to be
more careful with dates these days. Vikram had been a
close call. Great guy, but how could he have behaved
so insensitively towards waitstaff? She had read an
article about people like that. If they can be rude to
waiters, it speaks to their real personality when they
aren't on their best behavior. Needless to say, she had
never returned any of Vikram's calls since they went
out.

Now she had a new guy. She couldn't wait to
meet him tonight. Therefore, whoever this unknown
number was flashing on her phone screen, they had
better not be some telemarketer.

"Hello?" Jane answered the phone.

"Jane Jackson?"

"Who is this?"

"My name is Aisha Medina. I'm with the Black Gaming Network. You completed a form online and requested to be matched up with a buddy?" the friendly female voice on the other end introduced.

So much had happened since Jane's conversation with Ilana, the Director of HR at Gaming. Ilana had recommended that she join the Network. Jane went home that same day and filled out the online form. Apparently, she was actually getting a call for her efforts from someone at BGN.

"Wow. Thanks for calling me." She sat on her bed, eager to discover more about this affiliate group. "My mentor suggested that I join, and I confess, I'm really excited about the programs you have for people of color in the Gaming world."

"I'm so glad to hear that, Jane. Allow me to introduce myself and tell you a little about what motivates me to be part of BGN."

Jane nodded, "Of course."

"Jane, I should start by saying that though we have not met in person, yet, we at BGN are very down to earth and don't mince words about what we mean or say. So if I'm too direct for you, let me know, and I'll try to tone it down."

Jane felt excitement rush down her spine. "Aisha. Please. Be as down to earth as possible. I need to hear something genuine for the first time in ..." she paused. She couldn't remember how long it had been since she had received a dose of authenticity, so she repeated, "I need to hear something genuine."

"Good. As mentioned, my name is Aisha. I'm originally from Tunisia, Africa, and I'm an observant Muslim. My parents came to the United States when I was five, so really, I hardly know my African motherland but have always strived to remain connected to it. I have four identity traits working against me as I navigate American society: I'm Black, female, Muslim, and an immigrant from Africa." She paused. "Are you with me so far, Jane?"

Jane was enchanted, "Please, don't stop speaking."

Aisha laughed. She continued, "I'm a software engineer and I joined Gaming about five years ago. I wouldn't have survived this long if I hadn't joined the BGN. My career experience includes being on the receiving end of overt disparaging remarks about the way I dress; unconcealed innuendos from senior management about my 'incapabilities' in comparison to my non-Black colleagues; and, most of all, being passed over for promotion in favor of my younger, newly graduated colleagues who just happen to be prep school trained and considered more 'American' than I am. It's taken such a mental toll that I've had to consult a therapist within the last year."

"Oh, Aisha." Jane couldn't help but say it out loud, in sympathy.

Aisha went on, "It is unfortunately widespread across the company. For those of us who feel excluded or discriminated against, BGN offers a brief respite from all that. In fact, we have meetups for this. Have you been to one of these?"

"No," Jane admitted.

"BGN meetups are a place where we find camaraderie, a sense of belonging, an opportunity to collaborate on crafting solutions to the issues we're facing. Right now, given the issues I've raised, we are looking into documenting how bias manifests itself here at Gaming and how best leadership can address it with the expectation that HH and his veeps will use our findings and recommendations to take corrective action. We'd love to have your input, given your tenure here."

"Aisha. *Shukran*, for thinking of me. Consider my input 'had.'"

The other woman seemed to be smiling on the other end. *"Shukran?* Wow. Do you speak Arabic?

"No, only a few words that I picked up on my travels to Egypt a few years ago."

"Well, I'm still impressed. *Afwan*, Tiffany."

Jane smiled. "When may I meet you for coffee? I'd love to get to know you better."

"Very soon. *In sha' Allah.* I'll send you a calendar invite."

****

It had been an amazing call. She learned that BGN provided a haven and a space for Black people to discuss their experiences in the industry, how to handle the challenges they were facing, and, most of all, receive support and encouragement, knowing they were not alone. Not only that, they were looking to engage with leadership to effect change. She had to become a member, *pronto*.

The next meeting was scheduled for the following Wednesday. All members were expected to dial in from across the country. It was a conference of sorts. Jane couldn't wait. She made a mental note to make sure that Tiffany joined her.

In the meantime, she had a date tonight, and her nosy roommate was waiting in the living room as usual, all bug-eyed and checking out Jane's outfit.

"You look sleek," Leanne commented.

Her gray faux suede knee-length dress over her new green shoes had been carefully selected. She had seen this date's pictures multiple times, and she knew she was going to have a challenge feeling visible around a guy who looked so conspicuously fashionable in all his pictures.

She wasn't one to compete with a partner, but how do you complement your partner if they appear to be so striking? And he did look striking. Nice haircut with what most would call a caramel-brown complexion. He could pass for a Dwayne Johnson junior brother.

"Stay up!" Jane counseled her roommate. "I'm sure we'll have lots to talk about when I get back."

"You know me." Leanne spread herself out on the couch luxuriously and yawned. "I don't have a life, so I live vicariously through you. I will be right here upon your return because I must hear about your date!"

****

As she walked to the restaurant table, led by the host, Jane realized how right she was. He was every bit as attention grabbing in person as he had been in his pictures. He was well over six feet, like all her dates seemed to be. His sparkling white shirt was perfect against his skin tone, providing a shocking contrast that added to his appeal. He flashed a grin that revealed a dimple as he saw her approaching, probably recognizing her from her pictures.

"Jane. Hi. I'm Damian." He shook her hand with a dimpled smile.

Jane shook his hand and felt the warm pressure. "Damian, I'm pleased to meet you at last."

Chapter Twelve

Silvia ran her hairbrush through her thick, dark hair, her hand shaking. It was lunchtime. Barely ten minutes ago, she had been in Kyle's office. She was in the first-floor restroom, and in a few minutes, the lunch hour crowd would trudge into the cafeteria beyond the restroom. This room would soon start buzzing with ladies from the lunch crowd. She had to put herself together before then, with five minutes or less to achieve it.

Her shaking hand was representative of the rest of her body. She was trembling all over. Tucking her brush away, her shaky hands found the bottle of Advil stashed in her purse. She popped two in her mouth and washed it down with water from the restroom tap.

The door opened. Through the mirror, Silvia recognized the woman who just entered. Wasn't she that lawyer who was an HR Generalist? Silvia had met her only once during a lunchtime mixer sponsored by Gaming's executives. Yeah, she was Jane Jackson.

"Hi, Silvia!" Jane called out jovially and went into one of the stalls, shutting the door.

"Hi," Silvia mumbled. Good. Jane had not given her a double take. She must not look as bad as she felt. Kyle's hands on her were disgusting memories. She ran her fingers through her hair for the umpteenth time and rushed out of the restroom.

Jane was just walking out of the stall. "Hey, Silvia, you forgot ..." But the other woman was gone.

Jane washed her hands, noting Sylvia's small black purse sitting on the bathroom vanity. Poor woman must have a lot on her mind. "I had better find her before she freaks out about losing her stuff," Jane mumbled to herself.

She picked up the purse and a white piece of paper promptly dropped from it, as if it had been dangling somewhere along the edge. Jane frowned and thought to ignore it. Must be trash. No, maybe not. There was handwriting on it.

She bent down and picked it up. Jane. This is Silvia's personal stuff. You should not. Jane turned the paper over and saw it was a note, one paragraph long. Meant as a poem or song, possibly. It contained *words that her Mama would never have permitted her to read.*

She read. Her breath ceased in her lungs. She made a conscious effort to breathe again. It mentioned words such as *sexy. Hot Latina.* And *cock.*

Jane was too polite to read further. It was signed simply at the end: *Kyle.* She couldn't help herself. She took out her phone and snapped a picture of it. Jane stuffed it back into the purse and rushed out of the bathroom to find the purse's owner.

****

The huge TV screens that were prominently placed all over the cafeteria in the Venus building were intended to inform or entertain Gaming employees as they ate their lunch every day.

As Jane hurried through the rapidly filling cafeteria, she was not really thinking about the fact that there was a broadcast about to begin on the TV screens with the logo of a globally popular tech company displayed in the background of the conference center from where the broadcast was being shot.

She hardly noticed the round of applause as the keynote speaker of the event was invited to the podium. All she knew was that she had to find Sylvia and give the girl her purse. Jane came to attention with regards to the TV broadcast blaring through the cafeteria only when she heard HH's voice coming through the speakers.

"Some of you may know me; some of you may not," HH was saying jovially to the audience at the tech company where he was speaking. How coincidental that the Gaming lunchroom was broadcasting his keynote speech in real time, Jane thought drily. "I'm the Chief eccentric guy at a gaming company where we're nuts enough to believe we can host our competitors' products on our e-commerce platform and live to tell the story! I'm talking about our new expansion at Gaming taking the e-commerce gaming space by storm!"

Jane spotted Silvia as HH's voice droned on. She was standing in line with a tray of food, a simple looking salad. She had clearly not noticed her purse was not on her yet. She would notice when she had to pay for her food at the check out, for sure.

Jane hurried over to her. "Hey, Silvia," Jane tapped her on the shoulder, "you forgot your purse in the restroom."

"Oh. Silly me!" Silvia gave a sheepish smile. 'Thank you, Jane."

Jane didn't know what to add. Should she hate this girl or feel sorry for her? *It was obvious that Kyle was sleeping with Silvia. Was it consensual? Was it any of her business? Gosh, how did she find herself in the middle of this soap opera mad house that was Gaming?*

"You bet!" Jane stepped back and then walked away, her head spinning with different thoughts. Her cell phone buzzed in the pocket of her pants. Gathering her thoughts, she grabbed it and put it to her ear. "Yes?" she bit out, still slightly frazzled.

"Jane?" It was Tiffany's voice.

"Hey," Jane adjusted her voice tone. "I've been thinking about you, Tiffany. Did you try out BGN?"

"I filled out a form on their website. I think someone's supposed to call me from this point."

Jane nodded, finding a corner outside the elevators to stand. 'That's right. I did that and got a call. I think you'll really like it, Tiffany."

"Well, I'm going to do something a bit more drastic than join a support group since I'm being told I need to be on a 'Change Program' or face severance," Tiffany announced.

Jane sucked in her breath, "What?"

"Jane, I'm spending my lunch hour today visiting an employment lawyer's office."

Jane's heart raced, "Tiffany, are you at a lawyer's office right now?"

"I am."

"Girl, be careful!" Jane whispered fiercely.

Tiffany sighed, "Listen. I have to go. The receptionist here is beckoning me for my appointment."

With that, Tiffany hung up.

"Want to join me for lunch?"

Jane turned around to find her boss, Tracey, standing beside her.

"Um, yeah!" More appropriately, no! But what could Jane say?

She ordered some sweet potato fries and chicken strips. Why not? It was as reckless as she could get this lunch hour. She was, after all, having lunch with her manager. Best behavior would have to be the norm.

"How are things going with the DE&I campaign we talked about last week?" Tracey wanted to know, as she sipped a spoonful of her miso soup.

Jane had synced with Heather's team on this project a few times and they had come up with a list of initiatives, but that was as far as she had advanced on her collaboration with the DE&I team. "It's going well. I will send you a more formal update this afternoon."

"Good," said Tracey. "I have a new special task for you."

Jane braced herself. Now what?

"I need some research done on Tiffany's file," said Tracey.

Jane stared at her, "Tiffany Johnson? From legal?" she asked, just to be sure.

Tracey smiled, "Jane, I know we're a massive company, but Tiffany is the only Tiffany in the directory, at least in this building, right?"

Jane nodded mutely.

"I need to have you pull up the background information of her prior employment history and her record so far at Gaming. Could you handle that, Jane?"

Jane nodded mutely, like a robot.

She was at a point today where she couldn't really argue. She just had to do as she was told, so she had been told. What more was there to say? Wait. She did have something to say.

"Tracey. I found something. It looks like a poem or maybe a song? I don't know exactly but it's something along those lines."

Tracey looked at her with a quizzical stare.

Jane brought out her phone. She pulled up Kyle's note. She handed it over to Tracey.

Tracey read it. Her expression was bland.

"Send it to me," she said quietly, handing back the phone. "How did you come about this?"

"It fell out of Silvia's purse. She didn't know. I handed her purse back to her, together with the paper where the note was written."

Tracey nodded, "Good. We are HR. We remain discrete at all times. Right?"

What did that mean? She knew what it meant. It would remain discrete.

Jane emailed the note half-heartedly, miserably. If anything needed to be done for justice's sake, was there no one she could depend on around here?

Silently, she turned her head to watch the TV screen where HH was driving the audience wild with his typical charismatic diatribe of "technology rules the world and, hey, have you heard about Gaming's role in that space?" She had seen a few of his speeches since joining Gaming. It was like a firefly to a fire, drawn to something dangerous but too mesmerized to stay away because of its nature. Her nature was to find solutions. Find solutions to problems.

HH had become a problem for her sensitive mind, anyway. He grew this behemoth of a company. The culture of it had to be a carbon copy of his beliefs or personality. Otherwise, he would have made changes to it, would he not?

So she found herself binge-watching a lot of his speeches. There was a common theme: Technology versus Gaming's space in its declarations. Good for him. At least, it worked for his fame.

****

"Did you see the newspapers this morning?" Leanne poked her head into Jane's room where she was folding up some laundry on the bed before breakfast and heading out for the office.

"What? Who reads newspapers anymore?" she wanted to know, chuckling. "Everything is online now!"

"Well, we still get the old-fashioned delivery to our front door, Madame Twenty-First Century!" Leanne walked in and dropped a sheaf of newspapers on Jane's bed. "Read all about it! Your big boss is making headlines!"

"What?" Jane looked down at the papers discarded on her bed. It was face up, displaying the front page. And sure enough, Jane saw the big letters splashed across the heading:

Hans Husselkus and the Gaming V-Team

What technology has put together, let no man put asunder.

Jane threw down her clean leggings that were on the verge of being folded and picked up the paper, speed-reading it:

Hans Husselkus, the famous CEO of Gaming Inc., may be a gaming technology mastermind with top-of-the-class gadgets and gaming inventions to his name and credit but maybe it is about time he invented technology that would keep his emails secret. Last night, there was a massive leak of an email thread that Hans had mistakenly shared with his former female friend over the past few months. It is believed that this was not the handiwork of a hacker or some tech genius who knows how to leak company secrets. Rather, this appears, but this is yet to be confirmed, to be an intentional revelation. The former female friend forwarded the email to a few of her closest friends. Why did this former lady 'friend' of Husselkus do this? It would appear she felt heavily put off that she wasn't going to become the new Mrs. Husselkus as Husselkus had effectively decided to love her and leave her.

When Husselkus ended his association with his friend, one of her best friends was only too happy to let the media know about what she had discovered. After all, it isn't everyday that ordinary folk gain access to the private emails of gaming technology company moguls. So what did this secret email have to say? It had some highly damaging information about Husselkus's Vice President team. It alleges that three male VPs at Gaming had sexually assaulted their juniors and Gaming had covered it up by quickly settling with victims and making them sign highly restrictive NDAs. The executives were not castigated in any way, shape, or form by Gaming or Husselkus. We recently asked Husselkus for comment on these emails and here's what he had to say: "I value my V-team very highly. My relationship with some of them goes as far back as when I started Gaming. They have supported Gaming and I through thick and thin - so, naturally, I'm highly supportive

of them too. We have an unshakable bond. What's

wrong with having your own tribe?"

"Oh no, he didn't!" Jane declared.

"Oh yes, he did," confirmed her roommate who

was still hanging around somewhere by her elbow.

"How am I going to go to work now with a

straight face, seeing that Tracey and I have a meeting

with a couple of his precious V-team members today?"

Jane lamented. Work life was proving to be patently

unfair for the headspace of inexperienced recruits like

her.

Chapter Thirteen

Kyle's phone buzzed. He rolled his eyes as he tore his attention away from the tropical sea that spread out in front of him, a view that he could enjoy from the balcony of his seventh floor, five-star hotel room in Hawaii.

It was John. What was John calling about? Surely, he's able to handle business in the office? It was the purpose of being a delegate, right? Your delegate does the work you're supposed to be doing and doesn't call to bother you!

"What?" he snapped into the cell phone receiver.

"Hi, Kyle. Hope you are having a good time at …"

"Get to the point!" Kyle didn't want some eavesdropper that may be standing around John to hear that he, Kyle, was in Hawaii. "What is it?"

"Thanks for delegating your mailbox to me. Scot's email just came in, and he wants you to attend a BD meeting this afternoon."

Still irritated, he snapped, "Is that why you're calling me? Why aren't you getting ready to attend it?"

John hesitated, "I don't know the meaning ..."

"Yes?"

John stopped speaking, then picked up again, "I can handle it. *Ahem*," a generic clearing of the throat. "Hey, did you hear about the news in Seattle about HH this morning?"

"I'm not in Seattle, am I? How would I know? So what is it?"

John said animatedly, "Something about HH loving his V-Team like a mistress or girlfriend or something to that effect. It's got a lot of people buzzing in the office this morning."

What? That was such a tame comment. What were people buzzing about? It was no secret that HH was into his V-team, as they were clearly inseparable. Kyle shook his head, irritated, "Do you have any *real* news to share?"

John seemed appropriately reprimanded. "No. Thanks. Have fun. And bye."

Kyle shook his head again as he hung up the phone. What an incompetent kid. He had left the reins of the team to him for only three days to enable Kyle take care of some of his own business. Was that too much to ask?

He had opened a new LLC and it required a partnership with a large hotel chain. He had to speak with a general manager of a national hotel brand this afternoon and that was why he was in Hawaii. John had better not call him again. He was building his own personal empire outside of Gaming, and no one should interrupt him while he was on it. So what that it was on Gaming's time and dime?

****

John knew that there was sweat beading his neckline. He sure hoped it was not showing. Thank God he was wearing a navy blue t-shirt today. It would not be cool to be seen sweating bullets while in a meeting with the VP of Business Development, Michael Keep, and the project management nerds from the fourth floor. Marketplaces. Game Studios onboarding. Shifting deadlines.

"People, Project High is in final stages of deployment," Michael was saying. With a suddenness that made John's head spin, he turned to look at John. "John, what would be legal's take on having a times and materials section in the contract for the third-party online distribution platform providers we are engaging internationally?" Michael turned in the conference room to give John a point-blank stare.

John blanched. He was the only guy from legal in the room. The question was directed at him. By the VP of Business Development himself.

"I definitely think we should have a times and materials contract," John spoke rapidly.

Michael nodded.

"Yeah? Why do you think that? Is that relevant in an online distribution platform use case?"

John looked at the person who had spoken. Justin Filloy. The same Justin who had sent Kyle multiple emails that expressly read, "*Your recommendations don't appear sound in the context of how we do business here which leads me to conclude that you don't have your arms around our business and/or the applicable law.*"

On the spot. Justin was looking at him triumphantly, expecting an answer. So was everyone else in the room. All eight pairs of eyes staring at John.

"Well," John cleared his throat, "A times contract term would be ideal. I know that a materials one would be invaluable when added to the mix, too. So, yes, we should definitely have a times and materials section to the contract."

The room was eerily silent. Michael turned to look at one of the project management team members with a look of horror on his face. "Did no one invite Kyle to this meeting?"

"We did." Justin was the one who spoke again. "He declined and said John would attend in his stead."

The whole room heaved, "Ah." As if that explained everything.

John sat curled up in his seat, knowing that his navy blue t-shirt would be soaking wet with stress sweat by the time this meeting was over.

****

"Hi sweetie."

Jane let out a sigh intended to relax her gut muscles as she got off the elevator and picked up her phone on the first ring. It was Damian on the other side. Damian—her date, four outings in a row.

Maybe, just maybe she had lucked out on this one. Her third date-pick from LTRc, and she and Damian had already been on four dates. This was getting to be something. Okay, maybe by any stretch of the imagination, four dates were not all that. But it was better than her last two experiences with Duke and Vikram.

Damian was simply the big, Black athletic guy image who happened to be soft-spoken and open, and yet sometimes, it seemed to her as if there was something more beyond his ever-calm exterior that she'd not yet been able to decipher. Well, that was the purpose of dating. She would get to know him soon enough.

She replied, "Hey."

"What are you doing?"

Now how could she answer that? How could she explain that she would be spending her lunch hour this Thursday visiting the therapist that Aisha from BGN had recommended for her?

First, Damian didn't know that she was a member of BGN. And second, she was not about to tell a guy that she was heading into therapy. What did that bode for the future perspective about her mental health in the eyes of the date she had not known well enough to be telling such things? Maybe she could tell him about work diversity, equity, and inclusion shenanigans in vague terms but not this.

"I'm ..."

Just up ahead, Jane saw Carla Thunderhawk, the newest recruit of the legal department, waving at her. She waved back and ceased the opportunity to divert the subject about her upcoming errand of therapy from Damian's ears. What he did not know couldn't hurt him. She walked briskly up to Carla. "I'm just running into a lady from upstairs that I've been dying to speak to, so I'll be in a chitchat mode for a bit. You?"

He seemed distracted enough not to inquire further about the lady she had been dying to speak with, "So what did you think of my last text?"

Jane racked her brain. Uh-oh. Her phone battery had died that morning. She had been charging it up at her desk and only realized at lunch time that her phone had been off all day while it charged. It was possible to be unaware of phone status. She'd been in meetings all day with hardly a moment to mess around with phone hugging. "I was in meetings all day, sorry. You know how it goes at Gaming."

"Yeah, yeah. Death by meetings. You've mentioned. I asked if you're ready to go to the next level."

She stopped in her tracks. Carla was standing with another colleague and speaking casually, so Jane wasn't concerned that she was going to miss out on saying a word of hello to her. She seemed relaxed in place and not about to take off anytime soon. Jane turned back to her phone call. "I'm sorry, what now, Damian?"

"You don't know what next level means?"

Okay. She *so* did not have time for this.

"Are we talking about getting physical?" she inquired, to be sure.

"What else?"

She had never heard him speak so impatiently. What was up with the guy today?

"Um, did you read all of my profile on LTRc?" She stood still, as if she were required to get her words out. "I'm not climbing into bed like a common bed warmer without a committed relationship. That's the beauty of the dating app, right? All members can be open about how they want their relationships to unfold and at which stage of the relationship they believe it's appropriate to become intimate. I thought we were on the same level about commitment before playing married. Are we committed, Damian?"

He laughed as if he were laughing *at* her. She wasn't sure why it felt that way. "What type of commitment are you talking about? Like, put-a-ring-on-it-committed before we can ...?" He left the question hanging.

Okay, buster, let's see what you are made of. "Can you manage that?" she taunted.

He laughed again. "How many guys do you keep around with that ridiculous belief? Which man do you know that sticks around with a girl when she's not sleeping with him?"

She didn't know why she was so annoyed. So they had been on *four* dates. Was her value in a relationship or as a woman determined by her getting in bed with her date? Who made that moronic rule?

"You're saying I can't keep a man unless I sleep with him?" she wanted to know.

He laughed again. Clearly, he had no nuggets of intelligence to share. The laughter was a cover up for a lack of astute argument.

"Listen. I gotta go. If you're still into a sane relationship where we get to know each rather than mere bodies distracted by bedroom gymnastics, give me a call," and she hung up.

He was hot, but she wasn't going to rush into that with him or any other guy, for that matter. For some reason, that just blinds people from getting a good sense of who they are dealing with. Just look at Uncle Syl and Aunt Charmaine: Their relationship started out all hot and heavy, but now it was as cold as ice. Aunt Charmaine was miserable as sin. Nope, she was going to wait until she felt like she had a much better inkling of what made her partner tick. Maybe even up until marriage. A smile slowly crept into her face as she thought about how happy that would make her mom who had super old-fashioned and misogynist views about what men considered marriage material. "A guy won't marry you if you sleep with him, Jane," she'd often say. "He'll be thinking, why buy the cow when you can get the milk for free?" It was so old school, but her mom was adamant that she was right, no matter how much she pushed back against that sentiment. No doubt she would be thrilled if Jane waited. Jane wasn't really sure if she was inclined to wait that long, but she sure wasn't going to shag someone who wanted to move to that level so quickly. *Hasta la proxima,* Damian!

✶✶✶✶✶✶✶✶✶✶✶✶

"Jane, hi!" Carla was smiling as Jane walked up to her at last.

She was dark haired and what one would call dark skinned—a deeply tanned, petite lady with warm brown eyes and the sweetest smile. She had a dominating presence about her though. Maybe it had to do with the fact that her outfits were clearly never short of designer labels. Today, she was in a pinstriped shirt with a Gucci logo, her black pencil skirt was made of ciré, a nylon fabric made shiny by waxing and polishing. Jane couldn't recall which designer was famous for using such material, and as for her shoes, they were black pumps with golden "G" buckles, another Gucci brand, it seemed. Lovely but spending so much money on clothes was not Jane's style. Her mom had always said if you can't dress to kill on a shoestring budget, you probably don't have style. So she learned how to dress well on a limited budget.

"Hi Carla!" Jane smiled, and said hello to Carla's lunchtime companion, a lady called Belinda Onoh who represented another new employee from procurement. Jane had met her at the Sign-On orientation some weeks back. "Well, aren't we the newcomers club! I would love to have lunch sometime ..." she began apologetically.

"But we understand it if your HR rules keep you off limits from your 'business partners.'" Carla grinned. "Hey Jane, may I speak with you?"

Jane knew it was about five minutes past the noon hour and she needed to be at her new therapist's office within ten minutes. Good thing the office was a five-minute drive down the road. "Yeah, sure," she said graciously. She could spare two minutes.

"I will catch you in the cafeteria, Carla." Belinda waved. "See you later, Jane," and she took off.

"What's up?" Jane wanted to know.

"Tiffany."

Uh-oh. "Tiffany?" Jane asked.

Carla's smile had melted into a worried frown, "I'm concerned about Tiffany. There's some buzz around the legal floor that she heard some hush-hush racist and misogynist stuff, and now she's in some kind of trouble." She looked even more worried.

"Jane, I'm getting jittery about us little folk in legal. Heck, at Gaming! I can be candid with you, can't I? You're not just working for the big guys who need protection from us little folk, are you?"

Jane felt nothing but shame. Was that how the typical employee considered HR to be? Knowing that Carla had just joined the company within the last five weeks—she was quite spunky with her views, speaking so openly. The girl had grit, for sure.

"Carla, I'm here to support every employee in legal. Please be assured that Gaming opposes discrimination in all its forms and that we strongly urge anyone who has been subjected to discrimination or who is a witness to such to report it so we can address it." *Liar.*

"Oh. So can I ask, what is being done about Tiffany? A lot of her projects are getting assigned to me, like, a reduction in her workload, and you know."

Carla left the words hanging, "Here is the thing, Jane. I'm not complaining about my workload. Goodness knows, I've hardly anything to do up there, like the rest of us in legal. I worked 70 –80-hour weeks at my last job, and that kind of environment is what makes me feel *alive*. But even though I have lesser work hours here and would kill for more, it's not going to be at the expense of my colleague's job!"

Jane hadn't realized it had gotten so bad that even peers at legal knew about Tiffany's situation now. And she had no answer.

"Carla, I'm not sure what you've heard or what you think you know, but I'm not at liberty to discuss any employment-related issues involving third parties. If you have a question or need support with a specific issue relating to your work, please ping me. I need to dash to a meeting right now."

Jane felt her tummy dip. She couldn't believe she had just said that to someone who had confided in her, expressed genuine concern for her colleague, and prioritized humanity over money and status.

****

Her phone buzzed as she jumped into her car. She grabbed it without looking, "Hello?"

"Hi."

Jane froze.

"Duke?" she said out his name in disbelief. Her first date from LTRc?

"Hey. You gotta give me a grade for effort."

This was so not a good time. First, Damian and his freakish need-bedtime demand, then facing her colleagues and her inadequacies in truly supporting employees, and now a call from an ex-first date?

"I gotta go." And she hung up.

He texted right after. *"I just want to say that I'm sorry. I've been working on that. All right? Can you honestly tell me you don't have your own weaknesses, like sucking up to your family?*

What could she say to that? His text message had cut her right to the bone.

She was Black and invisible. Did that mean she had no biases, too? Can a person not be a victim of one form of bigotry and the perpetrator of another form on someone else simultaneously? If so, maybe she was a hypocrite for expecting others to be tolerant of her type of biases while being intolerant of Duke's at the same time. The subject was too uncomfortable to contemplate, so she never texted him back.

Chapter Fourteen

Beth Chung smiled at her latest, newest patient who was laid out flat on the couch in the office, as if she were ready to pass out, or simply give up on her day. She was young, tall, beautiful, and one of the BGN members.

Beth had many members from BGN as her clients. Did that say anything about the BGN members? That there was such a large number of them who paid visits to therapists like her? Not necessarily. After all, she had learned while growing up that everyone needed a therapist. Even a therapist needed a therapist.

Life is full of pain. People can mess you up and leave you emotionally wounded. Unforeseen circumstances can derail your hopes and dreams. Bad things happen to good and bad people alike. Some of these people consult therapists in hopes of finding a balm for their wounds. A wise therapist will feed off the patients' epiphanies and healing, and will, in turn, recover from their own pain.

"It keeps hitting at me all at once," Jane was saying, hand pressed against her head as she continued to lie back on the comfortable couch, eyes closed. "Beth, I know we just met ..."

"Don't give me the 'we've just met speech,'" Beth interrupted intentionally. The sharp cut off was meant to get the patient focused on why they were there. "Just spill it all. I'm listening."

"Okay, let's not talk about my dating life in this session. That would probably be weird enough, even for you," she suggested to her new therapist, "Let's talk about how very inadequate and invisible I am at my job that I can't influence people or change!" With that said, Jane spilled.

Her therapist didn't judge or criticize her after she spilled all the details about how she couldn't save her colleague from potential firing. Jane was surprised but maybe that went to show that she was harder on herself than she should be. Maybe only she considered herself deplorable for being unable to foster a positive work experience for folks like Tiffany, given her role. Speaking of Tiffany, Jane hadn't been able to reach her by instant message or phone all day. She hadn't seen her online on the company network all day either. Was that a bad thing? Was Tiffany still with them? She should know when people got canned, but then, maybe, some dismissals were more discrete than others.

****

Uncertainties and more uncertainties but overall, not a bad day at all, in and out of the office. As Jane gathered up her belongings out of her desk, she glanced around. The HR floor had emptied of employees, for it was after 6 p.m. now. The DE&I training she had been conducting in the Vermont Meeting Room downstairs had just ended. Her manager had not attended, so Jane had spent the one hour between 5 p.m. and 6 p.m. talking about the partnership that HR had struck with a third party to identify various minority organizations in the community and sponsor them with generous donations for their programs.

"In summary, this is the message we wish to convey tonight," Jane said to wind up her presentation. "We at Gaming aren't just diverse and inclusive; we are *empathetic* and inclusive. We know the data. Many nonprofit organizations are struggling to find sufficient funds for their programs. We are partnering with them so that they know they have the benefit of our management as a resource for their programs plus a share in our financial contribution pledge of $5 million. We are very in tune with our social responsibility."

She would have loved to wash her own mouth out with soap as she took the elevator back to her desk after her presentation. Social responsibility? Where was the evidence within the walls of Gaming? Specifically, why had Tiffany become so quiet? What had been said or done to her at the upper echelons of HR that Jane didn't know about? Was it about time that she found out?

Irritated, she went into Tracey's office to store the USB drive that Tracey had given her for the meeting tonight. It contained the PowerPoint slides and accompanying research documents that she had presented, and Tracey wanted it back in her office before Jane left for the day. She should have emailed it but Tracey was so old school.

Tracey was gone. Jane hated going into her office when she wasn't around. It felt eerie in there because Jane was still not sure that she had figured out her manager or the things she could or couldn't say around her.

She placed the USB drive on the desk and noted that the drawer next to Tracey's chair was a smidge open.

HR was the absolute last place where you'd want to leave drawers and filing cabinets open. The secrets that those drawers and cabinets could tell. *Secrets.*

Jane's heart raced. She glanced towards the office door. All was quiet. She was *so* doing this. She pulled the drawer open and peeked in. Performance review files. A file marked "Disciplinary action." Oh. Right next to it, another file was labeled *Female Compensation Statistics.* She couldn't believe Tracey was keeping physical files on all this but she was so

going for that. Whether it was the last thing she did on

Earth.

Jane took the file out of the desk and swiftly

leafed through it, keeping her eyes peeled for the

door. She knew the janitor was lurking somewhere

around. They barely paid attention to office staff. Or

maybe they did. She didn't care. She was reading this

– the final page of it, anyway.

Gaming - Deriving Value from Compensation Disparities

Data culled from payscale.com research

https://www.payscale.com/data/gender-pay-gap

HR Conclusion and Recommendation

The analysis of current compensation structures in the technology industry across various races provides a conclusion of the value proposition for hiring women of color. The average wage rate for a Black female employee is 0.97 cents for every dollar earned by a white male counterpart of the same job and qualifications. In an economy where corporate cost efficiencies are becoming more amplified, this research demonstrates the potential financial benefits of hiring Black females to roles with high-level responsibility classifications (i.e., manager and above) but requiring only a lower cost of engagement. HR recommends that Gaming adopt this compensation approach.

****

She quickly snapped a picture of that.

"Ma'am, can I come to take out the trash?"

Jane nearly screamed out loud at the voice. It was the janitor, standing by the door, looking polite and clearly clueless as to what Jane was reading.

"Um, sure!"

The janitor came around, emptied the trash can by Tracey's desk into her garbage bag and promptly walked out again.

Jane speedily returned the file into the desk drawer, ensuring that it didn't look like it was open this time as she slid it shut (so that Tracey wouldn't suspect that anyone had been aware it had been open all night).

Project High. It was the label on the file that her fingers touched as she rummaged and returned *Female Compensation Statistics* to its original spot in the desk.

Jane's eyes glued to the manila folder. *Oh no.* She wasn't walking away from *that.*

Project High—The new game that Gaming was deploying into the marketplace soon? There was an HR file version about it, right here in Tracey's office. She tugged at it. The red stamp across the front of the folder flashed before her eyes: *Strictly Confidential.*

It gave her all kinds of goose bumps when she thought of docilely complying with the file's stamped request to remain confidential. Like she had already determined when she was reading the lips of the VP of legal, Jeff Erickson and his guest, at lunch the other day, she was going straight to hell for violating confidences and privacy. Jane pulled out the manila folder, glanced at the office door again to confirm that all was quiet and started to scan through pages for what knowledge needed to get snapped with her phone.

Wow. A BRD was stacked in there. No time to stand about and read it all. She had already spent too much time going through the Female Compensation Statistics document. She didn't have that luxury with this one.

Besides, she knew the gist behind BRDs. Her buddy, Sarah, had been more than open with dispensing how Gaming's product development process was managed.

"The BRD sets out what the business is aiming to accomplish in the market. In our context, it typically sets out what the customer's pain point or need is and how the product or service we're looking to launch is going to resolve that; what is in and out of scope for that launch; when the launch will take place; what the launch dependencies are, if any; what the potential fast follow launch plans are; yada yada yada. You get the drift," Sarah had narrated in a sing-song voice, as if giving a tour to a bunch of bright-eyed, bushy-tailed high school students as they sat together for lunch about a week earlier. Sarah was such a drama queen. Jane had found herself only smiling as she allowed her tour guide to continue with her knowledge dispensation: "It also sets outs a press release around what the product would entail, and girl, those Gaming press releases get so dressed up, they would put a royal wedding in England to shame!" Sarah sipped on her soup.

"Press release drafted by BD folks? That's interesting. Why?" Jane had interrupted, curious.

Sarah shook her head. "It's funny but from what I can tell, they're not always distributed to the public, yet I always see them in BRDs I've had visibility to. I think they were initiated as a way to impel the BD folks to crystalize the benefits of a product or service as succinctly as possible. They serve as a helpful project summary not only for BD folks but for other teams as well. In the Project High use case, I expect that the press release will provide an outline of the game story. For instance, Project High is supposed to be ..." she dropped her voice, looked around surreptitiously as if there were eavesdroppers. Then she continued conspiratorially, her blue eyes wide and mischievous. "Project High is all about violent battles that take place between Black and Brown men in their hoods as they try to outdo one another in selling menthol cigarettes to kids and the babes on the streets that the players will turn their attention to from time to time as objectivized sideshows, if ya know what I mean?"

Jane blinked at her. "Sarah, if you were not a pal with no discretion about speaking her mind, I would have said you were insensitive for saying that outright just now. Don't you care about my feelings?" Jane had inquired dramatically. Okay, maybe it was a bit too much, her playing up what Sarah had told her.

But she was beginning to learn the art of deflection around these walls over the past several months. You hear something that hits you in the solar plexus? Deflect it with a little humor or sarcasm.

So males of color protagonists, sales of menthol cigarette to kids, female sexual molestation, and violence. That was Project High, in summary? How vile!

"Jane dear, you know I'm your sister from another mother, and I would never dare to hurt your feelings intentionally," Sarah announced.

"Girl, how do you know this?" Jane had demanded.

Sarah cleared her throat, "I've spent my four years at Gaming wisely. I know all the right people in low places—you know, juniors who attend meetings with their directors and veeps and tend to see and hear ... stuff."

Jane felt her palms go clammy. "Should we be discussing this?" she asked Sarah, her voice dropping down to a whisper. "Should we even know *about* what you're saying, Sarah?"

"Girlfriend, if you and I shied away from knowing the things we should *not* know around here, what else would be left to enthrall us behind these dreary walls?" Sarah wanted to know, uncaring, as she bit into a bread roll.

Jane shut her mouth. She allowed Sarah to speak on.

Sarah continued, "Like I was saying, the BRD will have all the juicy details about press releases for any project being developed. It will include projected financials for the product or service over a particular period of its life. The business tends to keep the BRDs very close to its vest. They are typically only shared on a need-to-know basis."

"Now I wish I could see it," Jane confessed.

"Yes, you and me both, sis," said Sarah.

"Who puts all that BRD stuff together, anyway?" Jane asked her buddy.

"The team assigned to the product's development," Sarah informed her. "They put it together and then get it reviewed by the senior BD folks and any other relevant big wigs. Once those guys sign off, the Head of Business Development and Head of Innovation Incubation sign off on it, too."

"Seems to go through a lot of hands," Jane observed.

"Necessary hands," Sarah reminded. "To make sure that there's alignment on all aspects that I mentioned well before launch. But folks in HR, like us, don't typically get to see these, and even your manager doesn't get to see such stuff unless there's some, well, HR issue that seems to be of concern around the product or service."

"Hmm. A game about some races selling hard substances to kids and females who are their comic relief entertainment. I can't imagine the issues that would be engendered by that," Jane said with an innocent look.

Sarah pursed her lips. "Hey, you didn't hear any of these from me. I'm only stating what came down the grapevine of the people in low places who happen to be in my circle."

"What else do your people in low places know about this Project High BRD?" Jane hadn't been able to hide her continued, growing interest.

"Well, like I said, it gets signed off by a bunch of hands and then shared with the FLAT teams, which happen to be part of several other teams that will help to bring it to launch. Did I mention that this is a super secret project?"

"We're all aware that it's super secret, yet *you* know so much about it," Jane wondered.

Sarah the wonder-of-information shrugged. "What can I say? People love telling me stuff. It would be so rude of me to deny them of the pleasure of doing so! Anyway, I also know that the FLAT teams that are involved in this project have been asked to sign mountains of NDAs before they can get their hands on the BRD and its associated documents." She leaned in closer, as if sharing the topmost secret of all. "Hey, I heard from my low-level peeps that all the veeps were high-fiving this whole Project High game story except for Ken Agrawal—the VP of Innovation Incubation."

"Really?"

"Yup," confirmed Sarah, as if she had been in the room and heard it from firsthand experience.

"Even though his team worked with the BD teams on this, he apparently took issue with this project but his underlings who play golf with HH went above his head and sold it to HH on the golf course. Ken personally took issue with the sale of menthol cigarettes to kids, even if it is in-game character kids, and how minorities and women are portrayed and said we shouldn't peddle discriminatory gaming products because it's financially advantageous to do so! I'm told no one paid any attention to him and that he may very well have hurt his career prospects here. Can you believe that? So *mashugana!*"

Crazy indeed. The pile of careers wrecked by "the powers that be" was growing at Gaming. Jane was certain hers would be joining that pile considering her present physical coordinates in the building, after hours.

Jane stood in Tracey's empty office as the conversation she had with Sarah about a week ago threaded through her mind. She looked down at the file in her hands. Yes, that was it, all right. It was marked "Project High. *Strictly Confidential.*"

"The FLAT teams that are involved in this project have been asked to sign mountains of NDAs before they can get their hands on the BRD and associated documents," Sarah's voice resounded in Jane's head.

Yet here she stood, holding that file in her hand. How *surreal.* Considering she was nowhere near the job role or level that would be allowed even to sign an NDA to get visibility to this in the first place. Excitement mounted in her.

Ten minutes later, Jane stashed the file back in its original location, aware that she had just used up a modest amount of memory on her phone to take pictures. She then fled.

****

8:00 a.m. Thursday morning. She was doing this.

Before bed yesterday, she had read every single word that she had snapped on her phone from the Project High file. Its contents left her so unsettled that she had tossed and turned all night. Her mind conflicted about what she should do. If she were a praying person, she would have asked for guidance. But as it was, she wasn't in the least bit religious. In fact, she wasn't even sure she believed in the existence of God. She did go through a seeking phase when she was younger and had, in that season, attended a church, shul, and masjid a few times. Her search came up empty though, and over the years, she became comfortable with her agnosticism. For some obscure reason, while tossing and turning, she recalled a teaching she'd heard many years ago about folks who were called to take on world-changing missions. Abraham. Moses. David. Isaiah. Esther. Folks who had responded with one heart to the call. *Hineni.* Here am I. Send me.

She couldn't believe she remembered that. It was so long ago. She wasn't sure she believed the texts on which the teaching was based, but for some reason, the memory spoke to some part of her. She knew she had a calling to guide people in their careers. If that calling meant she had to do something about what she'd read not only for Gaming employees but for the gaming community in general, then so be it. *Hineni.*

Besides, she was Black. She was female, and Black women have spearheaded transformation and led in the fight for abolition, suffrage, civil rights, and women's rights. She was going to speak for every human being who was undervalued like she was because when Black women lead, every marginalized community in America wins.

She had to get this out. She had to choose her words carefully, of course. But it had to get out. She pulled an electronic copy of the confidentiality agreement that was stored on her computer's personal drive, the one she had signed with Gaming when she joined the company and read it thoroughly.

Caution to the wind. She started the email.

****

To: Hans Husselkus; Fiona Banchetti
Sent: April 18, 2019 8:05 AM
Subject: Black Females and Compensation
From: Jane Jackson

Hans and Fiona,

I joined Gaming nine months ago as an HR Generalist supporting the legal team.

I've been inspired by the sessions you've led on and off the Gaming campus about Gaming and, more specifically, by the messages you've shared about our innovative culture and the significant role that each and every one of us has in terms of contributing to the revolutionary and innovative work we're engaged in here. It is in this spirit of this understanding that I'm writing to you both about HR-related issues and my thoughts on how we can foster an environment that helps employees thrive.

Data shows that employees thrive in a work environment when they feel connected, informed, valued, and trusted. Where this is in place, employees become more invested in their company of employ and more innovative. In my tenure in HR so far, I've become aware of two areas of opportunity in this space.

The first relates to a gender pay equity disparity document headed "Female Compensation Statistics" that I recently became aware of. The document outlines a study that was carried out by a third-party entity on women's compensation packages in relation to White men's. It calls for Gaming to hire Black women at a lower compensation package structure vis-à-vis White men's to take advantage of the disparate compensation structure for cost efficiency reasons. I believe there's an opportunity for Gaming to hold itself accountable to its DE&I commitments by addressing this issue and being a pioneer of equal pay in the industry. I would be pleased to look more into this matter with the appropriate contacts in our teams should my support be needed.

The second issue relates to Project High. I've come to understand that there may be some diversity, equity, and inclusion-related concerns that may need to be addressed as it pertains to the treatment of kids, depiction of females, and specific ethnic groups as subjects in the game. I'm concerned that the game, in its current form, wages war against our values and that it will exert a noxious influence on the gaming community. I believe that, as leaders in the industry, we need to set the tone for other companies to follow by driving a sense of respect for and worthwhile connection to others in the digital gaming space, not just in terms of the platform we provide but also in terms of the products and services we provide. I am currently working with the DE&I team on some of their initiatives and would be pleased to lend my support to any Project High DE&I-related reviews in the lead up to launch. Please let me know if I can be of assistance.

Thanks,

Jane Jackson.

HR Generalist.

She didn't think twice about it. She had to do

this. She hit the send button and sat back in her chair

and waited for fate to take its course.

****

From: Hans Hasselkus
Sent: April 18, 2019 8:10 AM
To: Jeff Erikson; Fiona Banchetti
Subject: FW: Privileged and Confidential—Black
Females and Compensation
Jeff, seeking your advice.

WTF???

—

From: Fiona Banchetti
Sent: April 18, 2019 8:11 AM
To: Hans Hasselkus
Cc: Jeff Erikson
Subject: FW: Privileged and Confidential—Black
Females and Compensation

Noob. Completely and utterly wet behind the ears.

Believer in the best in humanity. Leave this to Tracey,

Heather, and I.

—

From: Jeff Erikson
Sent: April 18, 2019 8:12 AM

To: Tracey Valentini; Heather da Santos
Cc: Hans Hasselkus; Fiona Banchetti
Subject: FW: Privileged and Confidential—Black Females and Compensation

+ Heather and Tracey

—

From: Fiona Banchetti
Sent: April 18, 2019 8:15 AM
To: Heather da Santos; Tracey Valentini
Cc: Jeff Erikson; Hans Hasselkus
Subject: FW: Privileged and Confidential—Black Females and Compensation

Heather, how's our DE&I campaign going? Get something out in the press *pronto* on how we're currently smashing our DEI targets and are looking to triple these targets for next year.

Trace, weave some yarn she'll buy about how we're looking into this and show her the door, ASAP! No "activist" replacements once she's out. Find us people who understand how businesses are run.

—

From: Tracey Valentini
Sent: April 18, 2019 8:45 AM
To: Fiona Banchetti
Cc: Heather da Santos; Jeff Erikson; Hans Hasselkus
Subject: FW: Privileged and Confidential—Black Females and Compensation

Sure Fiona. It'll be like taking candy from a baby.

—

As Tracey shot the email off, she kept her mind focused on the task. The usual activity buzzed around her office, but she had this to do. She needed to stay on track for promotion. Show the *bambino* the door. She could do that.

Her mind railed at the thought of it, over and over again though. Jane is just a kid. I mean, literally. She just got here. Now I get to show her the door?

She allowed her gut to stop railing at the idea. She needed to maintain a good record with the big folks. *I have kids to take care of. Besides, it's not my fault that this is a dog-eat-dog world. Don't hate the player; hate the game, Jane.*

Another email popped up on her screen. Hans.

She read it thirstily.

From: Hans Hasselkus
Sent: April 18, 2019 8:47 AM
To: Tracey Valentini
Cc: Fiona Banchetti; Jeff Erikson; Heather de Santos
Subject: FW: Privileged and Confidential—Black Females and Compensation

And find some prominent Black woman doing

something to uplift Black folks to give $2 million to

and get PR to share messaging about how we love to

hear of folks that are working on bringing people

together instead of dividing them.

—

Tracey let her breath out slowly. *Yes, sir.*

Chapter Fifteen

"You're back early," Beth Chung commented as Jane sat down on the couch, "That's good. You represent a subset of my clients who take their mental health very seriously."

Jane closed her eyes and massaged her brow. So she had been here only three days ago. Maybe she had more mental stress than the average Black girl. Maybe this session would reveal just how much.

"I found some data in my manager's cabinet," Jane confessed. "And I had to talk to someone about it. I lucked out that you had this lunch hour open, didn't I?"

Beth had that empathetic look on her face that some therapists wear to show that they were in sync with their client's issues.

"I'm listening," she said quietly.

"It's the usual data that we all know already," Jane said, looking her therapist in the eye. "Black women are paid less than most races. But Gaming is taking it to a whole new level. They're making a case for hiring qualified Black females due to the lower corporate cost. While I don't see how that can be reconciled with the need for the average manager to hire candidates from a similar race group or background, I see how this argument could be the reason why more and more Black women remain underpaid."

Beth waited for Jane's thought process to continue churning, allowing almost a few minutes before saying anything. "And what do you think you can do about it, Jane?"

"Well, I thought I was doing something worthwhile when I sent an email to the CEO and VP of Recruiting, HR, and DE&I about it," Jane couldn't keep the irritation out of her voice, "It's been a week now, and I've nothing but absolute silence from them!"

"Why do you think that is?"

"I'm just a lowly HR Generalist who isn't worth the civility of an email acknowledgement?" Jane suggested.

Beth gave her that blank yet engaged look that was geared toward not suggesting anything but allowing the patient to talk through their own thoughts.

"Why have I always thought of myself as invisible?" Jane wondered out loud.

"I don't know, Jane. Why?"

Jane was silent for a full two minutes.

"Because I'm from an impoverished background," she said quietly. "I'm Black, one of the most racially stigmatized groups on the planet. I'm female. Considered lesser than a man. Three counts against me already. Why wouldn't I be invisible?" she said softly.

The silence stretched in the air.

"Why should you be?" Beth asked quietly.

Jane looked up at her, as if hit by a two-by-four. Why should she *be* invisible?

Words swam in her head. Something that a gentleman, an influencer in the Finance space had once said during a speech he delivered to an audience of thousands:

Whatever you think you are, it's true.

Jane's brain spun. I think I'm invisible. Therefore I am. What if I'm not?

She looked at Beth. Beth gave her the bland, expectant look.

"What if I'm not invisible?" she asked quietly.

"You won't know until you start acting like you're not."

"Maybe Gaming makes me invisible?" Jane wondered out loud.

Beth replied almost instantly, "Then why are you there?"

The question hung in the air.

****

"Jane. There you are. Had a good lunch?" Tracey was walking towards Jane's desk.

Jane exchanged a secret look with her cubby buddy, Sarah, who quickly looked away back to her computer as Tracey approached.

Here comes another *tête-à-tête* in Tracey's office, their exchanged looks had said. What now?

"Yes. It was," Jane said and left it at that.

"Have a moment? Let's chat."

Jane followed Tracey into her office and closed the door. Her heart raced. Was it discovered that Tracey's office was the place where she'd found the data about women's pay? Had someone told Tracey about Jane's email to Fiona and HH?

"I got some feedback about an email you had sent to Fiona and HH," Tracey echoed the exact words running through Jane's mind as she sat behind her desk and looked at Jane.

Jane's mind was racing. She had sort of expected this, but she hadn't really figured out the exact words to say. "I wanted to share my thoughts on ...," she began.

Tracey didn't let her finish. "You went *over* me, over our director, and emailed the *VP* of Recruiting, HR, and DE&I and our *CEO*?"

Jane fell silent, unsure of what else to say.

"There's a reason I'm your line manager, isn't there?"

Jane nodded mutely, feeling like a little girl in the principal's office.

"And your ideas, ideas about the pay equity gap and Project High. Why could you not bring them to me? Isn't that why we're a team?"

Jane shrank in her chair. What was that word that kept popping up in her mind over and over again since that day she walked down Harvard's halls as a freshman amidst a sea of faces of students who were mostly, statistically, from family-funded prep schools, trust funds, and predominantly fairer skin?

Invisible. That was the word. Invisible. The story of her life.

The look in Tracey's eyes, the words that kept pouring from her mouth at this very moment made Jane shrink more into her chair because they didn't sound like the words of her having been heard on that email. They sounded ...

"What were you thinking?" Tracey's volley of words culminated in that penultimate point as Jane dragged herself out of the thought bubble she had immersed herself in for the last minute. "Tell me, Jane. Inquiring minds want to know. What was your *rationale* for writing an email to the *CEO* of this company and his *VP of Recruiting, HR, and DE&I?*"

Rationale? Jane could think of a couple: To speak up about the disparate treatment of Black women employees' compensation. To voice the despicable culture of undermining women in gaming and at Gaming. To ... Jane couldn't put a sound to the words. They remained buried in her mind. "I, I thought I was helping," she said in a small voice.

A picture flashed before her eyes. In five minutes or less, she was going to be escorted to her desk, and security would stand by as she cleared it and was led out of the building, amidst the shame-inspiring gazes of coworkers watching her embarrassing exit from her first job. Fired. In five minutes or less, she was *so* fired. Jane was sure of it.

"Helping?" Tracey bellowed the word, "Really? Overlooking the chain of command, disrupting executive officers' work with thoughts from your perspective that aren't properly vetted for approach, and expecting them to implement this bottom–up strategy, you think that was *helping*?"

Jane felt sick to her stomach. Maybe it was evident on her face that she was feeling very emotional now. Or maybe Tracey was suddenly hit by some angel of compassion.

Whatever the reason, her manager's tone softened, slightly, on her next words. "You didn't think it through, did you, Jane?"

She had. But she wasn't going to admit that. She made no sound at the question, choosing to stay silent rather than to lie.

Tracey waited. As if she wouldn't go on unless Jane said something.

Jane sat with hands folded in her lap. "I had some ideas that I thought I could share, that's all ..."

Tracey's watchful eyes were sharp. Suddenly, she sighed, cutting off Jane's words. "Hmm. Ideas are good. We value employees that come forward with ideas." Her voice had softened further. Jane tried not to think of the fact that she had just cut her off mid-sentence, though. Because Tracey sounded slightly more amicable, for lack of a better word.

Not that Jane considered it a bad thing to have emailed HH and Fiona. Indeed, she was aware that some line managers hated it when you went to speak to the managers above them about anything. It would seem Tracey was not one of those.

Jane had to do what she did, though. What needed to be said, had to be said. So she had said it to the leaders right at the top.

She tried to explain further without saying too much: "Gaming's industry ideas on recruitment and diversity inspired me to join the company. That's why I figured HH and Fiona would consider it to be right up their alley if I presented ideas around that subject. I was thinking …"

"Though ideas are good, there's a time, place, and process for airing them, you know?" Tracey's smile was still in place.

Jane felt her heart somersault. Okay. She had to remember she was, in fact, in some sort of danger zone. Not that Tracey's voice had sounded anything but civil.

Time, place, and process? So this was not the right time to bring up disparate treatment issues that affected employees like her and Tiffany? When would the time be right? Who would make that determination? "I thought a conversation about equitable pay scales in the context of Black women in the workplace is something that Gaming would value engaging..." Jane could feel the falter in her voice.

Tracey suddenly smiled. "Jane, of course. I know what you mean. While it took me by surprise, you did what you had to do for the sake of something ... progressive. I get it. I wish you had come to me first, though, Jane."

Jane felt the knots in her belly slightly easing. Oh. It was the chain of command concern. That was what this meeting was all about? Because Tracey was not sounding so scary at this particular moment compared to sixty seconds ago.

Tracey was leaning forward even more amicably. "It's why I'm here. I'm your line manager. When you have problems, you come to me. When you need to discuss a concern, you tell me. That way, we can work something out together and present a united front if, say, we need to go and raise it with HH and Fiona. See what I mean? Together."

"I, yes, Tracey."

"Yeah?" Tracey had a camaraderie look on her face. "We all need advancement and a way forward, on all subjects. The way we go about such progress is key. Some ways are more detrimental than others, right?"

The knot was back in Jane's belly.

"You've made such wonderful presentations for our projects and initiatives, Jane, that I must say, I am considering this to be one of your unique performances on idea delivery," Tracey said.

Jane positively balked, "You, you are?"

"But of course!" Tracey suddenly laughed. "One for the team, Jane! You presented an idea to the top because you had to do what you deemed necessary, and that is a brownie point for taking initiative. Well done."

"Tracey, Thank you." Jane didn't know what else to say.

What just happened at the beginning of this conversation? Because it sounded as if it never happened?

"So we're good then? You have no more ideas that you think you may want to share with me at this time?"

Did Jane imagine it, or was there a slight emphasis on the word *ideas* that just came out of Tracey's mouth?

Jane shook her head. "No, Tracey. Nothing to share."

"Okay!" Tracey rose to her feet. "Good." Tracey smiled, and breezily changed the subject as if the last few moments had not happened. "Are you coming for the corporate dinner party at the Rainer Club?"

The Rainer Club. It was on 4th Avenue in Seattle. Jane had never been there since moving to the city but had heard of its popularity for events such as weddings and receptions, including high-end corporate parties. The buzz had been in the air for weeks. It was the official night before the release of Project High and HH was of the view that a celebration was in order. So all employees with direct or close links to the project's launch were invited. HR was part of the list, of course.

Was she going to this shindig? Why should she go?

Jane got up from her chair as well, following Tracey's example. Clearly, the *tête-à-tête* was coming to an end. "I may not be able to make it. I have something going on tonight."

"Oh. What a shame." Tracey didn't appear convinced but shrugged anyway. "If you do change your mind, I hear there will be plenty of music, and the food, well, what can I say?"

Jane conjured up a smile. "Thanks, Tracey."

"Let's get back to the grind, then. I'm really glad we had this chat, Jane!" Tracey was all smiles.

Jane turned towards the door. It was only as she exited the office that the realization hit her. One minute, she was sure she was getting fired. The next, Tracey had blown warmer air, talking about a united front and yada yada yada. What was the true ending of that conversation? Was Jane still in trouble? Or had the "united front" ending diluted that evil?

Besides, all that talk about progress and ideas - Tracey hadn't said anything about HH and Fiona acting on Jane's *ideas* from her email.

Except that, what had Tracey said instead? *There's a time, place, and process for airing ideas. The way we go about progress is key. Some ways are more detrimental than others.* What exactly had just happened? Was all well? Or wasn't it? Why was her gut telling her to take that ending with a grain of salt? That it was akin to a gentleness that precedes a fatal blow?

****

Splash!

This time around, there were no ogling elementary school students watching her as she butterfly-stroked her way to the end of the large pool at the Mercer Island Country Club. She was alone. Alone with her thoughts.

Jane. You aren't what people think of you.

She pushed against the wall of the pool with her toes and glided back in the opposite direction.

You are who you think that you are.

She stroked back in the opposite direction, water rippling around her like a silk blanket, soft and comforting. It was what she needed after a day that included time spent in her manager's office, a time when she wasn't sure if she would have a job before the day ended. The situation had turned around sharply to Tracey becoming seemingly more *understanding* of why Jane had written that email. She'd left work with no further eventful situations. All appeared quiet and well.

Her email to the executives remained unanswered though. The word popped up again in her mind. Invisible. No. No. Again, no. *You aren't invisible. You are phenomenal because you're discovering who you are.*

Glide. Bop. Turn around and swim in the opposite direction.

You don't run and hide when people act out their biases toward you. You face them. You challenge them. You overcome them. I have to go to that party.

She climbed out of the pool, water dripping off her in rivulets, as if she had just been thoroughly washed from a layer of something that had held her back, and she was now stepping out of the waters, the waters of experience, the waters of learning … into a new skin.

She was going to the Rainer Club tonight. She was facing Fiona, HH, and Tracey head on. She wasn't invisible. She was just about to step into her own new world.

Jane grabbed her towel and simultaneously picked up her phone, lying by the pool. She punched the number she had never deigned to call back.

The phone was picked up on the other side at the second ring. "Hello?" said Duke Liang's deep voice.

"Hi, Duke. It's Jane. I know I have ignored you, and I'm really sorry for that. Maybe that's not good enough and I'll totally understand, if so. So this is super impromptu, but I, I'm going to a work event tonight. Would you be open to going with me? Companions are welcome. I know I'm giving you very late notice, but I ... think it will be fun and I, well, I really would like to see you."

"A work party? Fun?" He laughed. "I've yet to attend one of those but okay, Jane. Lucky for you, I don't hold grudges. So I'm in but only if we can follow this up with something more private and fun after. Deal?"

"Deal!", Jane replied, her face breaking out into a big smile. Duke. Wow. What a good-natured guy.

****

She stared at the rich bisque color of the mansion with sprawling green lawns. She still couldn't believe Duke had agreed to see her tonight. It was such an impulsive move on her part, but she was happy. No, grateful actually.

Duke opened the passenger side door of her ancient and somewhat beat up looking Honda Civic and climbed into the passenger seat beside her.

She looked at him, "You live here?"

When he had given her the address for where she should pick him up for tonight's dinner party, it had not occurred to her that the zip code was in the

Medina area of greater Seattle. She couldn't imagine any single person living in such a humongous place.

"My parents live here," he rectified. "Dad needed help with a carpentry project, so I've been here for a couple of days."

"Okay, don't tell me." She held up her hand. "You're the guy who hangs out with your parents on weekends because you're extremely family oriented." She blew out her breath.

"I'm family oriented. No, I'm even more so, *community* oriented. But," his voice cracked a bit, "I'm sorry that I was ashamed to introduce you to my friends. Not that this is an excuse, but how often do you see interracial couples of our kind together?"

She had to stop and think about that. Asian and Black? Hardly ever.

"I like you, Jane. From the moment of hello on LTRc, many moons ago. From the moment I saw you for the first time in person. You're like that girl who knows she can be anything she wants, including hanging out with a guy like me, but you never give yourself the permission to do so. And me, well, I've come to realize since I met you that I want a woman who thinks outside the box instead of living by family and community traditions because I've grown up all my life being afraid of family and what they would think of me."

It was a rather long speech. They were stopped at a red light and Jane allowed it to sink in, her hands pressed against the steering wheel, her eyes looking straight ahead.

At last, she spoke. "Are you ready for adventure, Duke?"

He sighed with relief, "You bet I am, Jane."

She hit the gas, "Next stop—The Gaming party at the Rainer Club where our adventures begin."

Chapter Sixteen

Silvia hated big parties. She knew she didn't look it. Yet she hated spotlights. And she especially hated being put on the spot.

"Silvia, I'm so tuned in to you. I just knew I'd find you here!"

She nearly jumped out of her skin at the sound of the voice.

Kyle had just walked into the ladies' restroom.

"Kyle. Are you drunk?" Silvia pushed the words out of her mouth. She was at the party tonight because Jeff and HH's new right-hand man and counsel had required them all to attend. She had hoped to avoid this at all costs. *This* being Kyle.

"No." Kyle shut the door behind him, a look that was part sinister and part repulsive on his face. "Why?"

"This is the ladies' bathroom, Kyle!" Silvia pointed out the obvious.

"That's why I locked the door on my way in."

Silvia stood helplessly in the middle of the bathroom floor. She knew all the stalls were empty. She was alone in here with *him*.

"Kyle, I need to get back out there ..."

"No, you don't."

"But ..."

"I said, no you don't!" he barked. "I'm your boss. You work for me. Right? You do as I say, especially if you want to get ahead and thrive here."

She nodded mutely.

"Good." There was malice in his eyes. "I've been waiting all night to see you."

****

"Well?"

"My mother would be proud of the shrimp platter," Duke observed.

"I'm not talking about the food, Duke," Jane rolled her eyes but felt a thrill of pleasure at having him beside her. There was another nosy person or other coming up to say hello. She could tell they only had eyes for the guy on whose arm she was leaning, "What do you think of the party? Quick, tell me, before Sarah, my gregarious desk buddy, and her fiancé, Phil Ackermann, get here. We won't be able to get a word in from then on."

"Not too shabby. We should do this more often, Jane."

She liked that. Sarah came up with her fiancé. Jane had met him at dinner a few weeks ago when she went on a night out with her roommate, Leanne, Sarah, and her fiancé, Phil.

"Jane. I thought you were skipping the party!" Sarah gushed, looking only at Duke.

Phil was more polite. He smiled at them both.

Jane got the point. "Sarah, Phil, this is Duke. My date."

"Jane has never mentioned you!" Sarah took Duke's hand and literally pumped it, "Good to meet you."

Jane couldn't have been more grateful as she saw HH and four of his VP comrades walking into the hall. Duke may be getting spared from Sarah's soliloquy tonight. "Look, the veeps have arrived," she announced. All eyes turned towards the entrance as HH walked in, flanked by his veeps as he smiled and waved at the applause that erupted throughout the hall.

"He's going to deliver a speech," Sarah predicted.

"How do you know?" Jane wanted to know.

"Read the agenda, girlfriend. I'm going to the bathroom for a bit. This executive *talk* had better be good."

"I'm coming with you," she told Sarah. Then she turned to Duke.

He grinned. "I think Phil and I will survive a few moments alone with the Gaming family. Right, Phil?"

The tall man grinned back at Duke. "You betcha, bro."

Sarah and Jane took off. "Well. Don't those two look like they've hit it off well?" Sarah commented. "You didn't let me ask the question because I could feel the daggers in your eyes the whole time. Where did you meet Duke?"

Jane knew the question was coming. She was happy to share. "On a dating app. It's a new one on the market called LTRconnect."

"Oh! I should have my cousin check it out. You two look so ... matched up. I think the app must have done a good job."

It was a question Jane had been asking herself ever since she picked up Duke in her old Honda tonight. This was only a second date with him, literally. Why did she feel like she had wasted so much time over the past few months with the other guys when, well, there was a Duke around that she had been ignoring?

Sarah pushed open the door to the ladies' restroom, "Well, when we get back ..."

She stopped speaking and let out a mortified shout at the sight before her eyes in the restroom.

Jane stopped short beside Sarah to see what she was looking at.

Kyle and Silvia. Silvia was bent over a bathroom sink. Her skirt up.

Sarah screamed again.

"Help me. Jane, help!" Sylvia's hair was like a halo of still-perfect disarray around her face, but there were tears in her gorgeous brown eyes, looking to the HR Generalist that she knew, "He won't let me go!"

Kyle looked up, an outraged glare in his eyes, "That door was supposed to be locked!"

Jane copied Sarah's earlier response.

She screamed, too.

****

From: Hans Hasselkus
Sent: May 2, 2019 1:00 AM
To: Jeff Erikson
Subject: Privileged and Confidential

Kyle Smith—WTF??? Contain. Your ass on the line otherwise.

From: Jeff Erikson
Sent: May 2, 2019 1: 02 AM
To: Hans Hasselkus
Subject: RE: Privileged and Confidential

Consider it handled, boss.

Golf at Sahalee Country Club next weekend?

****

Jeff looked at his phone for a minute, waiting for a ping from Hans. A minute turned to two minutes. Then three. Nothing. All right. Kyle needed handling. He got the point.

****

Jeff sat in the closed office with Ilana, Fiona, Tracey, and Scot occupying all the seats around him.

Kyle sat at the end of the table, his face as red as a beet, his eyes flashing various versions of offense and contrition, all rolled up into one.

They had all filed into the conference room almost ten minutes ago. It was 7 a.m. on Friday morning. It was a miracle that Kyle was there. Jeff had not expected him to be. Maybe he should get the show started and put him out of his misery as fast as possible.

"So, Kyle," those were the first words that had been spoken ever since everyone filed into the secluded room almost ten minutes earlier. "What was that all about at the Rainer Hotel last night?"

Kyle was leaning forward, elbows braced on the table. He shrugged, "I don't know. Frankly, I don't know why the whole party had to shut down just because ..."

Everyone waited for him to say more. He did not say more.

"What was going on with you and Silvia, Kyle?" Fiona wanted to know.

Kyle glared at her, "Wasn't it obvious?"

"Did she want to be there?" Tracey inquired quietly.

"Why wouldn't she?" Kyle fired back.

Tracey looked apologetic, "I ask because we've spoken to Silvia. She said no."

"Then, she's a bold-faced, lying ..."

"You can save the language and name calling that's forthcoming, Kyle," Jeff said shortly. "It really doesn't help the situation. Your behavior at Rainer. This is bad. Very bad."

"Is it Silvia's word over mine?" Kyle fired back.

Tracey spoke up, "Kyle. Jane Jackson came across something in Silvia's purse a short while ago. She took a picture of it. It was a sexually explicit poem or song. You had written it for Silvia. Something about a hot, sexy Latina and your, how shall we say, body member? Does it ring a bell?"

Kyle didn't respond.

Tracey sighed and shook her head.

Kyle spoke up. "Yeah? Is that why the whole bunch of you had to be at this meeting? I thought Scot was my new manager, Jeff?" he taunted.

"You'll get your chance with Scot," Jeff said slowly. "And me. In the interest of time, all decision makers needed to be in the room to talk this through."

"So what's the decision?" Kyle demanded.

Fiona spoke calmly, "Jeff will provide you with the full details."

With that, she looked around the room and then got up and left.

Everyone else followed suit until Jeff was left alone with Kyle.

The younger man was no longer looking so sure of himself. His eyes now matched the color of his complexion. Red.

"Jeff, you can't fire me!" Kyle begged. "I've got nowhere else to go. My dad already thinks I'm a ..."

"Kyle, stop." Jeff shook his head. "I'm sorry. I would keep you around. But what you did is so ..." He searched for the word. "Public," he stated at last. "There's no hiding this. There's no justifying it to media or the employees. We have to let you go."

A long silence followed. Kyle's head was hanging as he seemed to be thinking of his options.

"Okay. Where does that leave me?" he wanted to know.

"Scot will provide you with a glowing reference, Kyle. If asked, we will assert that we are letting you go because corporate restructuring, reduction of staff, that kind of thing, makes it necessary. I know that you'll be fine." Jeff's phone was buzzing in his phone pocket. Out of habit, with a frown, he fished it out and glared down at it. His brow picked up as he pushed a button on the phone to take the call, "Hello?"

His EA's voice squeaked from the other end. Okay, why was Linda sounding so squeaky? The woman had a deep, bold voice. This didn't sound like her.

"Jeff?" she squeaked.

"What is it, Linda?"

"Reception just called for you at your desk. The cops are here."

Jeff blinked. His mind raced to the places he had been, things he had done over the last few days. Wait, he had done nothing legally wrong. What the ...?, "Cops?" he asked carefully.

"Reception didn't check the phone tool for the latest information on Kyle's direct manager. When the cops walked in, asking to speak with Kyle, Jenny at reception panicked and called you. She got me, of course, since your desk phone forwards."

Because Jenny at reception knew exactly what had gone down at The Rainer party, the whole freaking Gaming knew. Receptions were modicums of calm and professionalism, so he didn't blame Jenny for panicking since Gaming had a frigging sexual assault live wire on its hands right now. Okay. Jeff mentally shook his head. Rational. Calm. Practical. That was what everyone needed to be right now. The cops were downstairs waiting to speak to Kyle.

He carefully ended the call after a quiet thanks to his EA and glanced over at Kyle. The latter had been staring at him with a half-crazed expression the whole time.

"You look like you have seen a ghost," Kyle observed about Jeff's newly pasty complexion.

Jeff's lips thinned. "You don't look half as good yourself, but hey, buddy, I'm afraid we will need to go downstairs."

"Downstairs for *what*?" Kyle snarled. Clearly, diplomacy and professionalism, including speaking to your boss in the right tone, were no longer a consideration.

"The cops, Kyle. The cops are here. Specifically, for you."

If his expression had previously been half-crazed, now it was full-blown one thousand wattage manic, "The cops? What do you mean the cops? Why the cops? What are they doing here? Why me? Why are they looking for me?"

"Kyle, calm down." Jeff was rising slowly to his feet, hands up.

Kyle jumped up too, springing away from Jeff physically, backing into a wall on the other side of the room, "What do you mean, calm down? And why are you looking at me like that? Huh?"

"Kyle, I've not spoken to them."

"I'm not going anywhere!" Kyle screamed. "You can't let them take me! You can't, Jeff!"

His voice was raised and it continued to rise with each of those words. Faces were looking in through the glass wall of the conference room that faced the hallway beyond.

Fiona was standing in the doorway as she opened the door, "Is everything okay?"

"I've got this ...," Jeff began.

"No! No, they can't have me! I'm not going anywhere!" Kyle was screaming.

"Ah. The cops." Fiona's face was grim. "You don't have to go anywhere, Kyle. I'll bring them up, then." And she exited the room, hurrying away to do just that.

Jeff let out a pent-up breath. *Okay, Fiona, you know that's worse,* he thought grimly. *Now, see what you are making Kyle do?*

Kyle had crumpled to the floor like a rag doll and was sobbing uncontrollably.

Chapter Seventeen

Two weeks later

John Putin stood in the middle of the empty office and let his breath out slowly. He couldn't believe he was here. He was standing in Kyle's old office. He was now the Senior Counsel for the legal team supporting the BD folks. Kyle was gone.

****

Tiffany covertly averted her eyes as she observed Jeff's glance in her direction the moment she got off the elevator on the first floor. She was certain she played it well. She knew how to avoid the higher-ups without their actually noticing that they were being avoided. Rushing through hallways as if late for some project meeting was one of them. Jeff stood with a couple of veeps, speaking quietly about whatever stuff veeps discuss with other veeps.

She wasn't ready to be on the radar of the management now. Or ever. Keeping her head down the past months while undergoing a most humiliating Change Program had been bad enough.

She couldn't fathom why John Putin had summoned her for a lunch meeting today. John, several years her junior in experience and years, was now her new boss. How much fairer could life get?

"Tiffany."

She found John seated at the table by the windows facing north in the cafeteria, the exact spot where he'd told her to come find him.

Tiffany didn't say a word in response as she slid into the chair opposite him with her tray of food. She wasn't hungry, but she knew she had to keep up the lunch appearance. A light salad and box of juice were on her tray.

"I would have paid for your lunch if you'd been able to join me sooner," John quipped, eyeing her tray. His tray of pasta was in front of him. Clearly, he had ordered before she got there.

"Well, John, I had that meeting with the BD team, which always tends to run over, so ..." She shrugged, eyeing his lunch tray. "Looks like I kept you waiting for lunch." It was 12:09 p.m. Nine minutes late to be exact. She didn't say she was sorry.

John was quiet for a moment, as if that was exactly what he was expecting her to say. A, "sorry I'm late, boss" type of apology. After all, he was now the boss. That's what you do. You make your boss like you by being as endearing as you possibly can. Right? When she turned to her salad and picked up her fork, he seemed to realize that an apology wasn't coming.

"That's okay!" he said quickly, as if to save his spurned expectation from further embarrassment.

"We all have meetings that run overtime. Kudos for taking that particular meet-up with Justin today, Tiffany."

She shrugged without looking up from her plate. It was akin to a *whatever* gesture. She did as she was told. She was, after all, on a Change Program now, thanks to Kyle, the exited nitwit. She was told to go for meetings; she went. She was given the lowliest projects to manage; she managed them. What is a girl caught in the middle of inequitable circumstances who doesn't have the resources to mount a legal suit back supposed to do?

"So, lunch. This is a first. I love having lunch on the team. Not that we had that really happen in previous times," Tiffany commented as she took her first bite of salad. The light jab was at the exited Kyle's management style. Aloof and dictatorial, as far as she was concerned. Now was a good time to fish and see what she should expect from John over his tenure of manager-ship. After all, even while he was a mere teammate in legal like her, they had never been to lunch together in his almost one-year time span of being at Gaming.

"Yeah. And a little belated, I must confess." John's plate of pasta looked like it was running cold since he was hardly touching it. He seemed nervous. Tiffany wondered why. "I love the opportunity to bond with our team, and we never really had that when, well, when Kyle was here."

Tiffany said nothing and took another bite of salad. What, talk about her former manager with her new manager? Awkward. She wasn't going down that rabbit hole.

John appeared to take the hint. "You and I seem to have gotten off on the wrong foot from the beginning, Tiffany."

Ya think? She thought it. She didn't say it. Instead, she commented, "I don't know if I would put it that way. We didn't interact much since we often were working on different projects while Kyle was the lead." She had to do it. Be diplomatic. Again, what can you do?

"Well," John looked embarrassed and she could tell he was bashful because she could see a tinge of red spreading across his cheeks. "I know you had quite an uncomfortable time with that snafu around Kyle calling you something ... unpleasant."

"You mean Kyle's racist commentary about my being 'an *angry hood rat*'?" Tiffany tossed her wavy hair back behind her shoulders. She had just gotten it done this weekend and was feeling especially confident today with the new look. Confident enough to goad her new manager into a talk about the nonculturally fit hood rat that Kyle had called her.

John's face colored further. "Tiffany," his voice dropped lower, "you know, Kyle was the only one during our conversation that evening who had such base ... persuasions. Jeff and I didn't say anything pejorative."

Tiffany said nothing. She nibbled on her salad. A minute of silence passed before she spoke again. "I know what I heard that evening. I'm pretty sure I heard all of you laughing in Kyle's office. About my being a hood rat and all?"

"Tiffany," John looked desperate to make her understand, "It was all Kyle. Well, he was my manager. You know how that is. You have to be mindful of their position, respectful."

She gave him a veiled look that, on the face of it, seemed like an acknowledgment of his comment, but beneath the surface, she wasn't sure if he could tell that it was her covert look of disbelief that she had just bestowed upon him.

Like, yeah. Suck up to your bosses. Including allowing them to erode your values, if you have any. Was that what he was saying?

"Listen, Tiffany," John continued, "I want you and I to be on the right footing. I honestly don't know what Kyle's beef with you was. If you heard every part of our conversation that night, then you must have heard that I commended the quality of your work and tried to get to the bottom of what his issue was. But Kyle is gone now. I believe you've met the Change Program requirements. Honestly, I'll even go so far as to say I don't understand why you were on one to begin with, so we'll be getting you off on that ASAP. Scot and I are aligned on this."

Tiffany looked up from her plate, "You are?" All right. He must really want something from her.

"Absolutely. Look, Jeff, Scot, and I believe you're an asset to the team. In fact, just the other day, and this is just strictly between you, me, and the gatepost, there was conversation around a senior management table regarding how bright your future at Gaming is looking."

She continued to listen, putting her fork down. "Bright futures are good." Who was she kidding? Disparaging comments and hood rat opinions would always exist. There was no degree of diversity, equity, and inclusion activism that would ever be able to take it away from secret conversations behind corporate walls.

But if, in the midst of all that, some top management was talking about her *bright* future, hey, she could join and play this game. It, after all, meant a bright future still existed for her, right?

John Putin had no business being the Senior Counsel lead of their team. He didn't know hoot about a plethora of legal processes, and he was, well, inexperienced, technically and otherwise. It was unfair.

But a girl had to deal with the cards she was dealt, right? Besides, who knows how the future will unfold. Look at what happened with Kyle. He was here one day and gone the next. Life and fortunes can change on a dime.

"Tiffany," John was saying, "You have deep technical skills and a breadth of knowledge about Gaming, our mandate, and our team. I am going to need your help in my quest to take legal to the next level on the corporate landscape. Promotion is in the horizon for you, if you're willing to support the team on this."

The team. Meaning, him. Tiffany leaned back in her chair, very interested in where this conversation was going. "Promotion?" she repeated the word out loud.

"You'll become a people manager. Silvia and Jag would report to you."

Hmmm. She could handle that. "I would need a big raise to go with that. One that's based off the compensation structure that I should have been at to begin with but for the pay equity gap and one that takes into account my new responsibilities, including that of managing folks. Managing people is a whole different ball game, as you know." She folded her arms on the table.

John smiled. He was relaxing. She was in. "Tiffany, of course." *Phew. She was going along with this.* His hide was saved. Again.

John knew he needed her. The BD Director, Justin, and his team raved about Tiffany. She was also well liked by the legal team. He was still getting his arms around everything and he had already had a couple more run-ins with Justin who just seemed to love to question his ability around legalese, processes, and anything else he could think of. With Tiffany as his right-hand woman, John knew he would be all right among those sharks. She would make him look good. This was going to work out well. Everything would be all right.

****

Jane threw the last of her belongings into the small box. She had just turned her laptop in. Her computer screen on her desk was black. Turned off for the final time. The desk was polished clean of pictures and knickknacks that she had used to decorate it over the last eleven months of her time at Gaming as HR

Generalist. Today, that journey had come to an end. She was embarking on a new one.

Sarah was waiting for her downstairs, not trying to make it a scene as she hugged Jane goodbye. So she intended to do it by the elevators, away from the eyes of their colleagues and managers. It amazed Jane how everyone kept their heads doggedly fixed to their computers, as if one of their colleagues had not just quit and was walking out from their society. Jane had handed in her resignation to Tracey two weeks ago.

The scene had been nothing like the prior time when she had sat in Tracey's office. In those former times, Tracey wielded all the power. She reprimanded. She ordered. She gave opinions. Now, the tables were turned. Jane was the one telling Tracey what she wanted. She was out.

"I'm leaving Gaming, Tracey," Jane had said even before she was completely seated in the chair across from Tracey.

Tracey's expression had turned to shock, "What?"

Jane placed a typed letter of resignation on the table. "I will send an email copy shortly."

"Jane? What's going on? Why this sudden resignation?"

Jane looked her boss in the eye. Maybe for the first time since she started working there. "I've learned a lot."

"Is it because of Kyle's note to Silvia that you saw some weeks ago or last night's fiasco at the Rainer?"

Jane had been shocked. Tracey was acknowledging it? She was dropping her HR discretion policy where no one gets to talk about anything they see or hear?

Maybe she should have quit a long time ago.

"I'm thinking of a different direction for my career," Jane said diplomatically and officially. "I need some time to think it through and come up with what I'm going to do next." The real truth? She was developing standards for the type of workplace culture that she could succeed and thrive within. Gaming was not *it*.

She was not invisible. She would not condone an employer that made her feel that way.

Tracey sighed, "Jane, I'm so sorry to hear that. You have become such a valuable member of our team!" But inwardly, she was happy that she was spared the horrible task of having to work Jane out of Gaming. She'd intimated to Jane, after she had sent that audacious email to HH and Fiona, that her future here was limited, but she figured she might have to put more effort into actually working her out. So Jane got the hint and she was choosing to head out now. Incredible.

Today Jane carried the box of her belongings out as she stepped off the elevator. Her box was light since she had hardly any belongings on her desk at Gaming. What she did have was enough fingers available to press "send" on an email on her phone. One she had drafted all of last night from her personal email.

It was a message addressed to Boomberg. It narrated her ten-month tenure as an HR Generalist at Gaming, Inc. She gave a long narrative on Gaming's disparate pay scales, bogus DE&I campaign, Project High, and spoke of her email to the VP of HR, Recruiting, and DE&I and the CEO about the pay equity gap and Project High and their silence. It was her way of trying to effect transformation. Her way of building on the work that was started by women who were caught up in #gamergate and, of course, by even more women throughout history going all the way back to the likes of Sojourner Truth. She was confident, that together, their cumulative efforts could, in Sojourner Truth's words, turn this upside-down world on the "right side back again."

Sarah was waiting for her by the elevator. Without a word, Sarah tucked an arm under Jane's arm and escorted her in companionable silence out of the building.

"So. What will you do with an entire rest of the day off? It's barely noon. Lucky you that you get to take off early," Sarah said warmly.

"I have the whole day, and tomorrow, and the day after to think through things," Jane said smiling. "I'm excited and can't wait."

"Yeah. Would that also have something to do with the fact that a certain tall, good-looking gentleman is waiting in a sparkling white BMW to pick you up?" Sarah tossed her head in the direction of the vehicle and the man in question as Duke stepped out of his car and began to walk towards them with a smile.

"That may have something to do with it, yes," Jane admitted, smiling as Duke came up quietly, nodded to Sarah, took the box from Jane's hands, gave her a warm hug, and headed back to the car to wait for her.

Sarah said, "*I'm* jealous."

Jane replied promptly, "And I, I *am* a visible Black woman who's not afraid to go after what she wants. Love you, Sarah. See you around."

Chapter Eighteen

Article from Boomberg.com

Getting High on Gaming's "High"

June 3, 2019

High—the latest multiplayer video game innovation by technology gaming giant, Gaming, Inc., has been causing a lot of waves in the market since its launch. Unfortunately, these have not been the good kind.

Jane Jackson, a former HR Generalist at Gaming, recently spilled the beans on all she uncovered about this controversial game in the lead up to its launch. What she witnessed led her to quit her job at Gaming.

"'High' objectifies women and glorifies violence against them," Jackson proclaimed in the

email she wrote to Boomberg. *"As if that isn't deplorable enough, it portrays people of color in ways that reinforce racial stereotypes. Black and Brown males are portrayed as brutally violent and sexual predatory men. The game also venerates addictive substance dealing, the sale of such substances to minors, and prison time."*

According to Jackson, the treatment of women and minorities in *High* mirrors how women and minorities are treated at Gaming. *'There's a ubiquitous 'White boy's club' culture at Gaming. Women and minorities are relegated to second-class status and are treated inequitably as far as compensation, project assignments, hiring, and promotion are concerned. Women and minorities are assigned to projects that don't garner senior management attention, are promoted at a much slower rate compared to White men, and only a handful ever reach the higher echelons of the company. Women, specifically, are also regularly subjected to the degradation and humiliation of sexual harassment."*

Internal documents leaked by Jackson to Boomberg reveal that the VP of HR, Recruitment, and DE&I, Fiona Banchetti, recommended that more women, Black ones in particular, be hired but not because she believes Gaming will benefit from a diverse and inclusive milieu but for cost-efficiency purposes as they would be awarded lesser compensation structures in comparison to those of White males for carrying out the same roles and responsibilities. The documents reveal that this recommendation was endorsed by Gaming's Founder and CEO, Hans Husselkus.

Jackson requested Hans Husselkus and Fiona Banchetti to look into addressing this matter, but her email was summarily ignored. *"The need to create an environment where employees of diverse attributes feel connected, informed, trusted, and valued is a matter that is often shut down by HR or leadership when raised. For instance, the Black Gaming Network, one of the affinity groups at Gaming, submitted a report to leadership outlining how bias is manifesting itself at Gaming, with recommended corrective action steps, but their recommendations fell on deaf ears,"* Jackson said.

Boomberg reached out to representatives of Hans Husselkus and Fiona Banchetti for comment, but they declined to do so.

Comments (10,158)

Reader123: So disgusting! What kind of a woman does this to other women and POCs?

Powertothepeople: Uh, a White one! Which planet are you living on?

Factsoverfeelings: Which part of "the recommendation affected White women, too" subtext didn't @powertothepeople get?! Some people are so daft!

Powertothepeople: Um, I'm pretty sure the article made it clear that this only affected Black women. Some people need English language comprehension classes.

Reasonrlz: She might be a VP, but she's a victim of the patriarchy system, people.

Choicesmatter: Oh, here we go with the blame "the man" game again! Did HH make this recommendation? Newsflash: White men are not responsible for all of your ills!

Powertothepeople: What's this @choicesmatter fool talking about? White men started this entire mess we're in.

Sistatosistalove: I see we're back to leaving White women out of the equation again. White women were codesigners of the mess. Did you know that they could, for instance, buy and sell slaves back in the day? Today, some still have their lot thrown in with White supremacy. I swear that in my next life, I want to come back as a White woman so I can play both sides of the game—benefit from employment equity to get ahead, on the one side, and blame White men for all the world's ills and tout the import of meritocracy, on the other.

Reasonrlz: Seriously, all White women?

Factsoverfeelings: Maybe Black people would do so much better if they would just take some f***ing responsibilities for their lives and stop blaming everybody else for why they're not prospering. We are living in 2019 after all. What's their excuse for not being able to get ahead? Black kids can't even f***ing read. Maybe they can start with getting that right in their community first.

Powertothepeople: Know anything about the history of this country, systemic racism, and how that's impacted Black people, @factsoverfeelings dips**t? There are structures that inhibit agency. Go pick up a history book.

Bigtechsucks: Folks, the buck stops with HH at Gaming. He's responsible for the misogynist and racist workplace culture and for the games and platforms that harm women, POCs, and the LGBTQ+ community. Didn't he also cover up all sorts of sexual harassment cases at Gaming? The guy sucks. HH has just got to go.

Powertothepeople: Down with HH. Power to the people!

Equalityforall: What @powertothepeople said.

Allyofthepeople: Hey, hey! Ho, ho! HH has got to go! So cheesy but I couldn't resist especially since comments here don't appear to be all that "high brow." Thought the platform was supposed to be? Lol.

Humanitylover: I heard Gaming employees have signed a petition asking for HH's head and that they're going to stage a walkout soon.

Munchkin20: What about Fiona? I'm with sistatosistalove on this one. Why does she get to get off scot-free?

Reasonrlz: You clearly are just clueless about the power of patriarchy.

Choicesmatter: And all white men are a monolith, right?

Powertothepeople: Did anyone say that all White men are racist? Stop with all that. We're talking about systemic issues here nitwit.

[Click here to load more comments]

****

Jeff only had to remember the first few lines of that blasted Boomberg article and he would break out in uncomfortable hives. At the moment, he stood even more awkwardly in the doorway as he watched HH look around the corner office morosely, as if checking to see the last knickknacks that he didn't currently have in the brown carton box that he held in his hands. Satisfied that he had everything, he hazarded a look in Jeff's direction.

It was Jeff's opportunity and opening to spew out his decidedly subservient words because, well, as far as he was concerned, HH would always be the boss. "I'm really sorry that this had to happen, HH," he said with sufficient regret injected into his voice.

"Really, Jeff? Middle-aged male with a voraciously ambitious appetite that has been eyeing the CEO chair ever since the first day I hired you, just like the rest of them other sharks? You're *sorry*?"

Jeff swallowed and gave it another shot. "It's not every day that a man lets go of the CEO reins. You built this company from the ground up. It's got to be sucky to be doing so under these circumstances."

"*Sucky*. Now, that's a word I would expect my twelve-year-old nephew to lug around." His clearly irritated glare made Jeff squirm slightly. "Having to unceremoniously step down as CEO is a rain on my parade. Anyone who was really intimately acquainted with me would know that."

But Jeff did know. HH *lived* Gaming. Being relegated to mere Chairman of the Board status must have been like a stab in his Founder and CEO ego.

"Hans, I know you may not believe this, but I understand where you're coming from." Jeff's lips were pursed in a thin line. "You're seeing red right now. I get it. I'll chuck your frustration with me right now down to the turmoil we've all been through. I know you know I didn't orchestrate this sudden turn of events. Your fury should be directed at that little HR rookie that we all kinda-sorta underestimated, like, say, three months ago. Boy, has she come back to bite us all in the behind!"

Jeff's forthrightness reached HH at last. He dropped his box of belongings on the big executive CEO desk that used to be his only twenty-four hours ago and folded his arms. "Yeah," he said quietly, "we underestimated that little diversity-tooting, email campaigning *bambino*, did we not?"

"We kept her email quiet."

"Well, that didn't stop her, did it?" HH retorted with deep irritation. "As of last week, 85 percent of Gaming employees were asking for my head. Can you believe that? The gall! And can you believe her audacity? Calling on Congress to regulate the industry and badmouthing Gaming all over BNN."

Jeff just vehemently shook his head.

The public response to the Congressional session and the BNN broadcast that followed it had necessitated an emergency meeting of the Gaming Board. It was during that meeting that Hans had brought a motion, which was ultimately carried and adopted, that he step down as CEO of Gaming. Jeff had heard the full gist of how this and the BNN story had gone down.

****

Two Weeks Earlier

Jane sat in the chair at BNN's studios feeling the heat of the studio lights upon her face. There was a time counter about ten feet away, behind the cameras, and it was rapidly reading 1:52 and counting down from there. She had less than two minutes before they went on air.

She was going on air. With one of the most famous news anchors at BNN. Janice Roth was in the seat across from her, exchanging some last-minute words with her producer.

Jane shook with excitement. She could not believe this. She was three months out of Gaming and here she was, sitting in a BNN studio chair. Telling her story—the Gaming, Inc. story.

Janice welcomed the viewing audience. She introduced herself. "Thank you for joining another episode of *Justice for the Masses*," she said as her smile widened and as she spoke into the camera. "On this evening of *Justice*, we have with us Jane Jackson, a former HR Generalist at Gaming, Inc." She turned to look at Jane. "Our audience is dying to hear about you, Jane, so let's get right into it. You're a Harvard

Law School graduate who took her first job at the leading gaming tech company, Gaming, Inc., not as a lawyer but as an HR Generalist," Janice smiled. "You resigned from Gaming about three months ago, and on your way out, leaked some highly confidential internal documents about compensation structures and the *High* game. Since then, you've spoken to BSNBC and GBN and," Janice leaned forward, "more recently, you were invited by the Senate Commerce Committee to testify as a witness about the discrimination, misogyny, harassment, and hate in the gaming industry. True?"

"All true." Jane nodded slightly.

Janine crossed her arms across her knees as she leaned forward again, "Tell me, Jane, why did you feel that it was important to testify before the Senate Committee?"

A momentary silence ensued as Jane seemed to mull over the question, as if pulling memories from different experiences and scenarios. Then she gave a deep, long sigh and opened her mouth to speak. "I was grossly disappointed by leadership that was speaking out of both sides of its mouth."

"Care to explain what that means?" Janice probed.

Jane looked at the host. "I joined Gaming because I had read so much about Hans's generous donations to the Black community and how he was looking to disrupt bias and discrimination at Gaming and in the industry. I was excited about that prospect. What would it do for women, minorities, the LGBTQ+ community, and differently abled folks if a big tech company such as this, with an apparently motivated CEO, was announcing all these change initiatives."

"It sounds like you were disappointed because the announcements were all show and no substance?"

Jane's face broke into a big smile that traveled all the way to her almond-shaped eyes. She smiled because Janice had hit the nail on the head. "That's dead on! It was all a PR stunt. Performative allyship, really. Let me back up a little and give more color on what I mean.

"There are essentially two issues needing attention in the gaming industry. The first is, we need to look closely at whose stories are being depicted in the published video games and what the impact of that is. If you take a look at that, you'll find that the industry typically develops stories that are centered around White, young, straight, and physically abled male protagonists. In the majority of stories that have been crafted to date, differently abled folks are not included or catered for, women are depicted as objects without agency, and people of color are hardly ever depicted as playable characters. Gaming's *High* is a classic case in point. Women characters are only there for male entertainment or abuse purposes and people of color are depicted in very stereotypical ways. These depictions are extremely harmful because they exacerbate the discrimination that exists in society. You know, Janice, every human being has an innate desire to be seen and heard. When we're seen and heard, we feel like we belong—that we matter—and that sense of belonging feeds into our sense of security. But when we don't see ourselves reflected in the media we consume or, worse still, when we see ourselves depicted in ways that don't honor our humanity, we tend to feel isolated and as if our lives don't matter. So it's very important that this be addressed".

"That makes a lot of sense, Jane," Janice piped in, her head nodding gently up and down. "What's the second critical issue that needs to be looked into?"

"Simply this," Jane replied. "What measures are being put in place to combat harassment, hate, and extremism on gaming platforms?

"You know, Janice, when we're talking about this, we need to keep in mind that when gaming companies create gaming spaces, they are not only offering up spaces where people can come together to play but they are also, in a way, offering a social engagement platform. There are pros and cons to that. One significant advantage of these platforms is that they give folks space to form meaningful connections with others. Some people have formed good friendships and found significant partners on these platforms. That's pretty awesome and I celebrate that. Unfortunately, there is another side to this "coming together" aspect. When folks get on these platforms, they don't suddenly assume different personalities and mind-sets about other people. People show up with all of the biases they hold in the offline world about people of color, women, LGBTQ+, and differently abled folks, and when they act on these biases, that restricts the ability of those folks to have enriching experiences on these platforms.

"You know, data reveals that almost 83 percent of gamers between the ages of eighteen and forty-five are harassed while gaming. When it comes to younger gamers, almost fourteen million experience harassment. What's even more horrifying is that about 8 to 10 percent of both categories of gamers are exposed to White supremacist ideology. The perpetrators convey their racist, misogynist, homophobic, and anti-minority religious rhetoric verbally over headsets while playing with others;

through the use of gametags or aliases that are racially offensive or anti-Semitic; through the introduction of game characters who are dressed in racially offensive gear; and via in-game chat systems.

"Harassment and hate must be addressed so that everyone can feel safe and valued. Since gaming companies created these spaces, it's incumbent on them to ensure they're doing the hard work of fostering healthy interactions. We're not really seeing that though. Industry players, like Gaming, are issuing statements on social media that give the impression that they're seriously concerned about these issues, but they're really not willing to do the work of changing norms on these spaces or of taking action against the perpetrators. For instance, Hans Husselkus approved the design and launch of the reprehensible *High* game, and he and his leadership weren't interested in ensuring that Gaming's Online

Code of Conduct was augmented to combat discrimination, hate, and extremism."

"So that's what you meant about how they're speaking out of both sides of their mouths?"

"Exactly, Janice!" Jane said, "But, in the end, no one should be surprised that this is happening because industry players are themselves currently not diverse, so the biases of the majority of industry player developers and leaders are showing up in their innovations. When I was at Gaming, I was mandated to work on a radical DE&I program. It made the company look good on paper, but it did very little to advance inclusivity and equality. It was all initiated as some sort of pre-emptive defense to legal suits or communication to the effect that discrimination is condoned by the company."

"I get it. So this is what you wanted to convey to Congress?"

"That's right. I was motivated to testify for two reasons. One, to persuade them to intervene and put legislative measures in place that will prevent companies from developing gaming products or services that, like *High*, are harmful to women, kids, ethnic and religious minorities, and the LGBTQ+ community because it's clear we can't trust gaming companies not to violate the rights and dignity of others in their quest to grow their bottom line. Two, I wanted to implore them to mandate industry members to publish, on a semi-annual basis, data that speaks to the harassment and hate-related complaints they're getting and to outline their recommended corrective steps so that we can have transparency on the extent of bigotry and hate that's happening online and how they're addressing it, if at all."

"So what you're essentially saying is that gaming industry players need to spend less time talking about these issues and more time on working to address them effectively?" Janice enquired.

"Precisely. We know that they have the brainpower to do so. They're using that to create super innovative games and gaming platforms. I'm hard-pressed to see why they can't employ it to find creative ways to resolve these issues. Right now, the great majority of industry players are just publishing policies they don't even enforce. Others, like Gaming, are so resistant to changing norms that they haven't even started doing that yet. This needs to change because unabated hateful speech can very easily transform into hateful action. I'm hopeful that Congress will provoke that change."

"Hmm," Janice turned to the camera. "I noticed that after your testimony to Congress, you posted an update under the hashtags: #regulatehate and #humanityoverprofit."

Jane smiled at Janice. Then she looked at the camera and said softly, "Humanity over profit. That's all we are asking for."

"Our time's almost up. Any final words for Gaming, Jane?"

"Do better. If you want to be known as a company where everyone, regardless of their background, thrives, you have to put your money where your mouth is at. Address the pay-equity gap issue and pay employees who are working extremely hard for you what they are worth. Take a closer look at the Black Gaming Network's recommendations on how to stem bias and discrimination out and work with them to effect change. Folks see through your commercials on major TV networks that run for days on end showcasing projects being led by one or two people of color and your PR showcasing the millions of dollars you're pouring into marginalized. A best employer to work for reputation can't be bought; it must be earned. So, roll your sleeves up and engage in the kind of work that will ensure that every employee is seen, valued, and treated equitably at Gaming."

****

Jeff watched Hans pick up his lone box of belongings again as he looked around his beloved corner office one more time. The office that was now, officially, Jeff's office.

"Hans, we're going to miss you," Jeff said with a slight smile, extending his hand for a handshake and realizing belatedly that since Hans's hands were full with boxed belongings, he would likely not be able to shake hands.

Jeff should not have bothered. Hans snarled at him, "Drop dead while taking all the glory for my hard work, Jeff-boy. My eyes are on you from the lofty heights of the Boardroom, kid. Don't screw up."

And the ex-CEO stalked out of the office.

Chapter Nineteen

Well done, Jane Jackson. The same words from fourteen months ago echoed in her ears. The words had rushed through her as she launched into the warm waters of the Mercer Island Country Club fourteen months ago. Words that congratulated her diving prowess.

Jane dived into the pool, slicing through the surface like a knife through butter. *Well done, Jane.* This time, the words congratulated her for *life*—the life she had lived these past fourteen months. The people she had become acquainted with. The experiences she had gained. The storms she had weathered.

Like a picture frame in the clear crystal of the pool waters before her eyes, faces floated before her—Tracey Valentini, Joe Olson, Jeff Erikson, Fiona

Banchetti, Hans Husselkus, Kyle Smith, and more. She, like the youthful, inexperienced David facing several Goliaths who were warriors of the corporate world and who could sink any unsuspecting rookie who dared to trouble the waters of their world. She had not been sunk. She dared to think; *she* sank *them*.

Jane sliced into the pool, the waters around her ankles and arms rippling with waves as if confirming the disturbance that she had caused in real life in a corporate environment that was in need of disruption. She had faced them all. She had challenged them. *Finish the race.*

The Voice suddenly reverberated in her mind. That same familiar Voice. The Voice that had been speaking to her from the beginning, from that day when she took her graduation walk in the auditorium of Harvard University.

Had she *finished* the race? Declan Anderson. The lawyer and influencer, the man behind the modern-day civil rights for Black professionals' movement, the man she had followed through high school who was the reason behind her decision to go to law school, the man who had been invited to her class graduation as the keynote speaker—his words had never rung so true.

Her arms minced through the pool waters in semicircular arcs of the breaststroke.

Finish the race.

She pushed at the wall of the pool with her foot. *Stroke. Stroke. Splash.* Her body glided backwards as she turned back like an eel towards the opposite direction of the pool. She arched her arms as she stroked back in the original direction from where she had started.

Did I finish the race, Declan? Jane whispered to his voice in her mind.

Kyle Smith—fired.

Hans Husselkus—stepped down, effectively fired.

Gaming's discriminatory and unconscionable policies and practices on minorities and women— exposed.

Boomberg, BSNBC, GBN, BNN, and a number of other media—broadcasting the exposé.

Congress—reviewing the efficacy of industry regulation.

Be unapologetic. Stand tall. And stand proud.

The Voice spoke in her head. She could see again, the enthralled audience, listening to him as he paused between each of those phrases to let the words ring into the hearts of those hearing them at the graduation ceremony.

"Four hundred years ago, you were without a voice." Declan's voice spoke in her ear. In her memory.

Splash! Stroke. Glide. She dominated the pool. She owned this realm.

"Today, you are one of the strongest voices in America."

Tears stung her vision as she stroked towards the edge of the pool. She had to get out now. She was feeling so overwhelmed with the *very* possibility that she had a *voice*.

Stand tall and stand proud. Declan's voice faded into the distance.

Dripping, she rose out of the swimming pool, wearing her one-piece black swimsuit with the insignia "H" stamped against the left side. She toweled herself dry. Jane Jackson sauntered out of the swimming area.

Standing tall. Standing proud.

About The Author

Lindi Tardif is an author, tech startup founder, board member, and an international tax lawyer with extensive experience in the corporate world with blue chip companies, including a Big Tech one. Lindi's diverse career has led her across the globe, from Johannesburg and London to Boston and Seattle. Lindi earned a Master of Laws in taxation degree from Boston University, as well as Bachelor of Commerce, Bachelor of Laws, and Master of Laws in taxation degrees from Wits University.

Lindi was born in Soweto, South Africa, where she lived under apartheid for twenty years. She is a third-generation activist and second-generation lawyer and writer. Her dad, a civil rights attorney, was murdered under the apartheid regime and her paternal granddad, an anti-apartheid activist and writer, spent over two decades in exile from South Africa under apartheid. Lindi currently lives on Mercer Island, Washington, with her kids.

CPSIA information can be obtained
at www.ICGtesting.com
Printed in the USA
LVHW080311030322
712511LV00013B/594